T0193938

THE ULTIMATE
VICTORY

ONYEMAECHI EMMANUEL OKORO

authorHOUSE®

AuthorHouse™
1663 Liberty Drive
Bloomington, IN 47403
www.authorhouse.com
Phone: 1 (800) 839-8640

Published by AuthorHouse 10/28/2017

ISBN: 978-1-5462-1438-0 (sc)
ISBN: 978-1-5462-1436-6 (hc)
ISBN: 978-1-5462-1437-3 (e)

Library of Congress Control Number: 2017916359

Print information available on the last page.

A nation should not be judged by how it treats its highest citizens, but its lowest ones.
—Nelson Mandela

None of us would die and rest in peace if we should leave this world without making our places better than we found them.
—Onyemaechi Emmanuel Okoro

This book is dedicated with enormous affection to my brother Honorable Eberechukwu-Bona (as popularly called), who has been my angel. He's an exceedingly loving person. And in memory of my spectacular friend and mentor, Professor James Strazzella, a man of indescribable and infinite kindness. I'll miss him dearly. Also, in remembrance of Father Lawrence Augustus Vallimont (CR) for his compassion, prayers, and formidable support of me.

ACKNOWLEDGMENTS

I appreciate my wife and children for their love. I thank my cousin Dr. Matthew N. Ibewiro, whose most profound and unmatched support renews my strength in times of need. I am especially thankful to Dr. James Nwachukwu, whose corrections and loving guidance improved the quality of this book. My immense appreciation to Dr. Ifeanyi Emma Mmagu for all his encouragement and kindness; and Ricky Moore, who has always been there for me. I am passionately appreciative to Father Livinus Ugochukwu–Aka-Nchawa, for all his prayers and support; my father-in-law, Joseph Offor; Monsignor S.E.U. Osigwe; Father Cyprain Chidi Osegbu; and Father Benjamin Nwanonenyi for their blessings and prayers.

I lack words to express enough gratitude to Dr. O. Ugo Anusionwu (Action Man) for what he has been to me; I pray that the almighty God will reward him abundantly.

I am grateful to my maternal uncle Cletus Nwoha for all his blessings and prayers, and to Chief Eddy Ekeanyanwu and Simon Iwunze for their loving care and support; and my wonderful friends and other people I treasure with esteemed regards: Judge Dr. Anthony Rulli, Bishop Dr. Micheal Emele, Jude Oseke, Ifeanyi Reginald Nwachukwu, Onwudiwe Anthony Ebo, Basil Nwokeke, Godfrey Offor, Celestine Agwu, Engr Vincent Aligwara, Sir Evarastus Anoruoh, Emma Onyemaechi Odoma, Albert Osigwe, Dr. Professor M. Iwunze, Chukwudi Chris Iwu, Sir Tony Anosike, Jude Egwekwe, Athanasius Agwu, Attorney Kevin Nwokorie, Sir Athanasius Ebelebe, Sir Felix Osuji, Ike Okoro, Dr Matthew Onuoha, and many others I could not mention here. God will continue to bless you.

All errors in this book are completely mine.

AUTHOR'S NOTE

This book was inspired by my reading of the books and other pieces of literature listed below, and listening to speeches, jokes, music, and more:

Julius Caesar: Shakespeare
Poor People's Movements: Frances Fox Piven and Richard A. Cloward
The World's Great Speeches: Lewis Copeland, L. W. Lamm, and S. J. McKenna
In Our Own Words: Senator Robert Torricelli and Andrew Carroll
God's Best Gift in an Ugly Wrapping: Onyemaechi Emmanuel Okoro
Man's Search for Meaning: Viktor E. Frankl
House of the Dead: Fyodor Dostoyevsky
Murder Trials: Cicero
Hold the Dream: Barbara Taylor Bradford
A Letter to Dr. Nnamdi Azikiwe: Mokwugo Okoye
A Hero of Our Time: M. Yu and D. J. Richards Lermontov
Power to the People: Laura Ingraham
The Discourses: Niccolo Machiavelli
The Republic of Plato, Translated by Francis Macdonald Cornford

CONTENTS

1

THE DREAM

Ed was seriously considering running for the presidential election coming up soon. This was not the first time he had had the urge to run, but in the past, he had never been able to get himself fully prepared to engage in the necessary election activities. He understood politics involved all kinds of intricacies but needed courage to take the first step. He had good friends who would give him strong financial support without minding how long and costly the entire process would be.

With all these assurances, Ed seemed to be ready to make a strong campaign. He began to articulate his plans, expecting to get all the necessary support from friends and associates who had always supported him in the past. The expected resources would make him highly competitive and create the advantages to win the primary and general elections.

One of the crucial aspects in running an election of this magnitude was, Ed hoped, getting a very strong support from family and close associates. Money would be essential but wouldn't determine everything. He knew it required a lot of traveling for the campaign and other political activities, including expensive advertisements. Though he was relatively popular among newspaper readers, being a staff writer for one of the regional newspapers, his popularity would not reduce the hassle. He needed to know the prospective candidates challenging him and how to balance their efforts. He also needed to understand the protocols involved in the political campaign. It might have seemed too early to worry about those problems, but it was important to be fully ready for them.

Ed slowly started to make preliminary consultations with some elders, friends, and political pundits in the community to explore their interests. He didn't want to inform his wife and children until he was completely certain he would run. Everything looked good, especially from those who said he had the charisma and conviction to get votes. His old friends promised to help in his fund-raising activities. A good number of the people he met encouraged him to run. That was exactly what he wanted to hear as he was getting more energized.

"It seems like people were waiting for me to make this move," he said to himself after receiving assurances from his friends, old and new. "I am going for it. I will give it my best shot, and I don't want to disappoint those who have such great confidence in me. I'm never a quitter. A quitter never wins."

Having rallied good support, he was ready to reveal his plans to his wife and children. Though he thought and believed it was time to tell them, he wasn't sure how his family members would receive the news. After deep thought, he concluded that doing it after the family dinner would be the ideal time. He later narrowed it down to a Friday at dinnertime because his wife would be home during the weekend. It would give him ample time to have conversations with her if she disliked the idea.

On that night, when everybody was almost done with the dinner, Ed announced that he had important news. "I want us to discuss, as a family, my ambitious adventure," he said.

All of them sat back and threw their attention on him.

"What's the ambitious adventure?" his daughter asked.

"I notice how curious everyone is. Yes, this is a big one. I'm sure I wouldn't do it without your full support. It is going to involve every member of the family in many ways. I mentioned last week that we would have a family meeting, but nobody expected the issue we are going to discuss. That's the real surprise," he continued.

As he was talking, the room was quiet, as if all of them were holding their breath. The movement of his legs under the table was heard loud and clear.

"Did you all enjoy your dinner?" he asked, trying to soften the tension.

"Yes," they responded quickly and in a chorus.

"Good."

His wife was looking straight at him without blinking. "Everything all right?" she quickly asked.

"Sure," he said, smiling. "I want us to discuss, as a family, my ultimate desire, which might take this family to a different level. I am considering running for the highest office of this great country: the presidency. If everything works out, and if you all would jointly support me, it would be a smoother and better journey. I want to know your honest opinions, which would help me conclude my preparations. Nothing is definite now. I am feeling strong about it, and my chance of winning this election is fabulous."

"Cool!" his young son said.

"What's cool?" his wife snapped at the little boy.

It was quiet again for two minutes. Everyone was looking at each other.

"Honey," he asked his wife, "can you say something? I know you would like to be called the first lady."

The kids laughed out loud, but his wife didn't manifest any emotion. She bent her head as if overwhelmed by such sudden information.

The whole room was deadly quiet like a graveyard. The three children had their eyes on their mother as though waiting for her to break the ice.

Ed sipped a little water from his cup before calling on his wife again. "Honey. Honey! Are you all right?"

"Yes, I am. I think we have to sleep on this issue before any person can reasonably say anything. It's a big surprise to me, but I need to take enough time to reflect on it."

"How much time do you need? Till tomorrow or the next day?" Ed asked.

"Just give me this weekend."

"Sounds good to me," he told his wife. "And to you kids, nobody has something to say except Junior, who said, 'Cool'?"

They all laughed again. His daughter, who was nineteen years old, responded that it would be better to wait, as their mom suggested.

"Good. I will take it."

All of them went their respective ways. And his wife, Titi, went to her bedroom. She looked confused and seemed eager to talk to somebody. She was a very private person and wouldn't be comfortable with the exposure that went with being in politics. Her husband made it clear that his plans were still at the embryonic stage, but her concerns were still high. She thought she'd like to be kept out of it completely, if possible.

Ed sat in the couch with his second son, watching television. He was looking at the television, but his mind had wandered away. Suddenly, he took a deep breath, as if he were trying to suppress his feeling. His son asked if he was all right, and he answered in the affirmative. Ed asked for a bottle of spring water, which his son quickly brought from the fridge. He didn't drink the water. It was left on the table, as if he had forgotten that he had requested it.

Titi struggled with what to do. She later decided to call her dad, who was also her mentor, to seek his advice. She closed the door so that her husband and children wouldn't hear their conversation. Her voice was almost inaudible, and she was almost choking with emotion.

Mr. Chucks, Ed's father-in-law, was a quiet but intelligent person, a retired professor of sociology. He was a nice man—and was good in deescalating tensions. Instead of discussing the issues with his daughter over the phone, he invited her to his house. He told his daughter that he would prefer to sit with her to have the discussion.

Titi agreed.

Ed was waiting for a second opportunity to continue his discussion with his wife and children. He was not a regular politician, although he had engaged in politics a lot with friends. There was a lot of speculation about how his wife would react after the consultation with her dad. Though he didn't say it, Ed was determined to run irrespective of his wife's position. He would prefer his wife to participate actively. He knew she would be considering the financial risks, especially the using of resources needed for their children's schools, knowing politics was a game of chance. Friends easily became enemies when proper care was not taken. No permanent friends, no permanent enemies.

The next day, Titi went to her dad, who was waiting for her. Her face showed her concerns. She related what her husband was planning to do and how he had explained his plan to his children at dinner.

"I have difficulties digesting this proposal because we have not been a political family," she told her dad. "My husband attends events now and then, but I never knew he was motivated by such a formidable ambition. I don't want him to think I'm stopping him from running, but politics has never been my thing."

"Well, it happens," her father said. "Prospective political candidates always make up their minds before telling their family members. A lot of people interested in politics do not tell their spouses for fear of being discouraged. This may be part of it.

"It's not easy to decide to run for public office, especially for the office of president of this country," he added while holding his daughter's hand and walking her to the kitchen table, where they sat face-to-face. He offered her peanuts, bananas and other fruits, and other snacks kept on the table.

"My daughter, do not hit the panic button yet," he said. "I don't blame you for any concerns, but the game has not started. Your husband is like a baby who should learn to walk before thinking about running."

"What do you mean, Dad? He has decided to run for the office of president."

"That's exactly what I want to explain to you, my daughter."

"Go ahead, Dad!"

"Your husband is figuring out whether you and the children would support his desire to declare his candidacy. Many other people would be interested too. And before declaring his interest, he would need to make some exploratory contacts, like having some town hall meetings and going to other public and private gatherings. Those would help him evaluate how people would react to him or say to him. That would help him measure his likability and decide whether to move further or quit early to reduce costs."

"Would he need fliers?" Titi asked her dad.

"No and yes. No because it is still too early to talk about fliers. He would be at the level of meeting immediate and extended community members to know how they feel about him and if they would support him. People could like him as a person but not as a leader. There could also be others who would be glad that he was running. Likeness has categories, but he would never know until he stepped inside. Yes on another aspect: fliers would enhance his popularity. When people started to know him, that would be a sign of progress, and his chances of being in the race would become more obvious. Then he would need more fliers."

"It's amazing that he would have to go through all that to become a candidate," Titi interjected.

"The marathon has not started," Mr. Chucks continued. "He would come to get advisers and hire agents who would direct him and help him navigate through difficult issues he would encounter on his way."

"I don't think we have the means to pursue this dream now," Titi said. "He should wait! It's a lot of hassle," she added.

"If he asked me, I would advise him to start from the House of Representatives or the Senate. Trying for the local council chairman would also be good. The presidency is really a heavyweight fight that would need national recognition. If you are not nationally known, you need a lot of resources, including financial donors, and strong party bigwigs to define you."

"Thanks, Dad," Titi said, and she kissed him on the cheek. "You have said it all. The more you explain these protocols, the more my head spins. Sometimes, these things seem easy when you see other people doing them. I will go back to further this discussion with my husband. I have a clearer view of where we are going and can give him a better opinion."

"Good luck, my daughter."

"Thanks, Dad,"

"I'm here for both of you at all times. If you want to come again for further discussion or want to come with your husband, that's fine with me."

"Definitely—we will do that if he insists on running."

She waved goodbye and left. On her way home, she stopped at a neighborhood shopping mall to get some things for the family. As she was coming slowly from the parking lot, she walked past two men and a woman who were talking at one of the mall's resting areas. She overheard them talking about Ed and the election.

"That's my husband," she said to herself while stopping involuntarily. She went closer to them, pretending to look for something in her bag as she eavesdropped. She wanted to know what they were saying about her husband.

"Ed would waste his hard-earned money if he tried to go for the presidency," one of the men said.

"You never know," the second man responded. "In politics, you never say never. He should take his chances, and if the people believe him, he will become the president."

"No," the first man said. "He's a good man as far as we know. I like his opinions in the newspaper, but he would not be a good politician. He's never run for any office before and has not been tested. He can't become the president from nowhere."

"But is he qualified to run?" the woman asked.

"Sure! If he has money to burn, he has all the constitutional rights," the second man replied.

"I know he's a staff writer for one of the local newspapers and also an attorney," the first man said.

"That's true. But none of those would help his candidacy," the second man said.

"Lawyers are good in politics," the woman said.

"Not all of them," the second man said. "Even with that, he should start from the ground up, like the Council, House, or Senate, before going higher. He could also try for the governorship. What type of magic wand does he have that would make him the president of this country now?"

"I wish him good luck," the woman said.

When Titi thought she had heard enough, she left without saying anything. She entered the mall to do her shopping but was eager to get home to meet her husband. Now she was more troubled than before. The things she had heard outside the mall struck on her concerns and made her wish her husband wouldn't get involved.

"How are you all doing?" she asked her children while walking into the house.

"Welcome, Mom!" they responded in chorus.

"I hope everyone is ready for our discussion with your dad tonight," she asked.

"I don't have much to say other than promising Dad my full support," said her daughter.

"Me too," said the first son.

"Me too," her second son said. "If he wins, everybody is moving into the president's house at the capital. And people will see us on television."

"It would have been wonderful if all of you had kept your opinions till your dad came home. You would be able to advise him better."

They noticed that their mom wasn't excited about it, and they stayed quiet. She kept quiet too.

Although Ed was eager to hear from his wife and his children, it didn't stop him from contacting more friends and seeking their support. He traveled to a neighboring state where he met some school mates and old friends. Despite a few of them having concerns and encouraging him to consider running for the Senate or the House as an alternative, the majority supported him and promised to campaign for him. He didn't want to hear anything other than to move on.

He came home determined to persuade his wife to go along with him to accomplish this burning desire. "It is something new for all of us, stepping into the political arena, but a journey of a thousand miles starts with a step," he assured himself. He thought about raising a lot of funds and borrowing if needed. He didn't believe it would be a stumbling block.

When it was time for dinner, everybody was available and ready to talk. Ed finished his food and readily waited for the others. He didn't say anything, but his body language announced that he was eager to start the conversation. Titi didn't seem to be in a hurry. After a little delay, and when everyone was ready, Ed began.

"I hope you all enjoyed your dinner."

"Yes," his children answered in chorus as if it was a funny question. He laughed while looking at his wife.

"Honey," he said to her, "what are you considering doing now? You must have acquired enough opinions from people, and it is time for us to decide as a family what to do."

His wife took a deep breath as if she were still confused about what to say.

"Say something," their daughter interrupted. "I am with Dad for anything he decides to do."

"Me too," the second son said.

"Me too," the first son added.

"That's really disrespectful to jump into my conversation," Titi said. "Since you think your opinions are more important, go ahead; I am out."

"No, honey. Sorry. Kids, you should apologize to your mom," Ed corrected them. "I appreciate your support. All your support is extremely crucial, but we can't do much without your mom's consent."

"Sorry, Mom," they said together.

"Good," Ed said. "Let's go on, honey. I don't think they mean to be rude to you." Then he added, jokingly, "It was overexcitement at the prospect of living at the president's house at the capital."

Everybody laughed.

"Darling," Titi said, turning to her husband, "on a more serious note, your ambition is wonderful and would make the family proud. You know how much I support all the things you do. But this time"—she paused for a long moment—"I think you're taking on more than you can handle. A new swimmer starts from the shallow water and progresses to the deeper part as he improves his skills." She paused again as if she expected her husband to intervene.

"Politics is like a mirage," she said. "The closer you get, the more it disappears. Worst of all, wasting your little savings and other resources for such a magnanimous dream may not be the best idea now. However, I am ready to go along with you if you must do it." She paused again, choked with emotion.

"I think," she continued, "preferably, if you would start with something lower, it would be more bearable and reasonable."

"How low do you mean?" Ed quickly asked his wife.

"You could start from Council chairman and go to the House or Senate. You have political friends but have never been involved directly by running for any office. Politics is a rough game, and one has to be ready for the intricacies that come with it. Am I making sense?"

"Sure," Ed responded.

"I encountered by accident a group of people at this neighborhood mall talking about you. Though they had different opinions, their consensus seemed to be that you wouldn't be a good politician. My dad almost had the same opinion. He seemed to think you are going too high at this moment. You should start with the lower offices up to the governor before climbing to the top to lead the whole nation. I agreed with him."

"You can be the president of the Senate," his daughter suggested, and all of them burst into laughter.

"It sounds good," Titi said. "My second opinion," she continued, "is to have some town hall meetings to understand firsthand how people feel about you."

"Thanks, honey, for your great opinion and invaluable discoveries." Ed kissed his wife on the cheek. "Thanks, kids, for your wonderful contributions. I love you all," he said, looking at his children.

Ed left and went to the living room, sitting quietly on the sofa and resting his head in his hands as if he were assimilating everything he had been told. His wife came up and asked if he wanted the television turned on, and he said no. The rest of the family members went to their respective rooms, leaving Ed alone in the living room.

Titi felt distinctly relieved, thinking she had removed a big load from her head after the conversation. "I may sleep better tonight," she said to herself while going to her bedroom.

Ed did not manifest any disagreement with what his wife had said. However, it has been said that politics is like alcohol: when you are addicted to it, it takes a while to get it out of your system.

As Titi was thinking she had watered down her husband's burning desire, she didn't know that the ruin and turmoil of politics was just getting started. No matter how you tame a lion, it's risky to unleash it with its teeth and nails intact. Everything that had been said to Ed didn't seem to discourage him, but induced him to think of the alternative.

He later started making calls to his friends, trying to figure out what to do next. One of his friends, Jack, suggested a meeting—a caucus, of sorts—to put their logistics together. Ed thought it was a good idea, and asked Jack to fix a date that would be convenient for him and their other friends. Both of them agreed to make more calls before deciding on a date.

After processing everything in his mind, including the earlier involvement and pledges from his friends, Ed was emboldened to stay on it. His wife had truly and affectionately outlined her position to him, and he didn't want her to feel ignored. He thought strongly about commencing with the town hall meetings. "The most valuable advice is what you get from the people who sincerely tell you the way things are without minding how you feel about it," he said to himself. "Friends could flatter you just to make you happy without giving you the true picture of yourself."

When Ed met with his caucus friends, every one of them started suggesting what to do and how to kick off the campaign. Some of them thought it would be good to start with fund raising, whereas others thought it was too early to do that since he had not fully made up his mind what to do. They reviewed other important opinions.

"Gentlemen, I am so proud of you for taking out the time to be here," Ed said. "Most of you could have been home watching sports or doing other things of more importance, but you chose to be here; I am humbled. It shows a deep commitment to get this thing right from the beginning. I couldn't have been happier than having all of you around me at this unequaled moment of challenges. Each and every one of you has made different wonderful contributions, and your ideas and opinions will be the most legitimate and meticulous weapon that will determine the success or failure of this endeavor. I have some other friends who will join us at one point or the other, but at this level, you are the chosen few. Let me allow you people to keep the ball rolling."

A man named Willie said, "I would appreciate it if we could streamline our plans starting with the town hall and other small-group meetings across the towns to appraise the ideas being presented to us. Some of us would not be available at certain gatherings. The most important person now is Ed, who needs to go around and establish that he is the people's person who is close to them and capable of solving both their individual and their national problems."

"Good point," Ola said.

"Agreed," Jack added. "But we should be asking people which issues will be important to them during this election so we can tailor our strategies appropriately."

"Absolutely right," Ola said. "Ed has the advantage of being in a lone front at this moment. He can use this opportunity to launch his proposals before other candidates start coming out."

CONSULTING FRIENDS

"Wonderful," Tom said. "The puzzle is gradually coming together. Let's start from the tri-states and move progressively to other areas as we weigh the pros and cons of our activities."

"Fabulous," Ed said. "If we maintain this dynamic manifestation, it will be an ultimate triumph. However, I don't want to take too much of your time today. Can we meet again at this same place and time next week?"

They all agreed. After a little more time drinking and chatting, they departed.

Ed seemed happy, and believed they had achieved a lot. He started getting excited and expected to continue from where they stopped when they met next. He went home but didn't discuss the meeting with his wife.

The second meeting was a follow-up to the first, as planned. Unfortunately, only three people were in attendance. The other two called to excuse themselves but promised to attend any other scheduled meetings. Ed explained everything to his friends in attendance, and none of them had a problem with it.

When the first town meeting was scheduled, Ed asked his friends to give their opinions, which would help him address some important topics and make a powerful impression.

"It is important to note that this town meeting, being the first, may be a little challenging," Ola said. "People's reactions and mode of asking questions will not be comfortable if they're not carefully handled. Sometimes, some constituents will question you as if you are the cause of any problems they have. You must control your temper and be able to navigate your way out. You could also go there without encountering any problems. The two important concerns that could come up from the communities will be crime and education. You have to be prepared to say something reasonable about those issues."

"I agree," Willie said. "You have to give the impression that you know their problems and are the person they should trust to solve them. Because you want to be president, you should be presidential in the way you talk and look. There must be a smile on your face at all times, and you must wave at people as you look in their directions. Be free to call any of us when you have questions. I know your profession prepared you for this call, but in politics, small things can easily escalate to big issues, and vice versa. No matter how this first encounter goes, it will be a stepping-stone, and you will learn from it. I am highly optimistic about your performance."

After a few more conversations and socializing, Ed thanked them again for coming. He asked everyone to spread the news about the town meeting so that there would be a good turnout. They left hoping to meet at the town hall venue.

2

FIRST TOWN HALL MEETING

There was a big crowd, which surprised Ed and his friends. Though Ed was the first prospective candidate to start campaigning, he wasn't expecting such a big crowd at the first town meeting. His friends who came with him were excited about it. They didn't care who or what had attracted all those people, but they were almost certain it wasn't about Ed alone. Ed was just a lawyer and a local newspaper staff writer who had developed an interest in politics.

As the townspeople were waiting patiently, Ed came out from behind the curtain to kick off the meeting.

"Hello, ladies and gentlemen," he started.

"Helloooooo!" the crowd responded.

"What a beautiful day! I am honored and privileged to be with you this evening. A lot of you don't know me because I am not one of those regular politicians who go on the radio and television to make promises they will not keep. I am an ordinary member of the community who, like every one of you, has questions about what our government is doing with our tax money. My intention today is for us to interact and begin to think seriously about whom we should send to the capital to take care of affairs during this coming election. This is a very important moment for us to turn things around and elect someone who will go to the inner cities and listen to the problems of their people. I am running for the office of president and can assure you that you have in front of you the best man for the job. I am not here to make long speeches but to be with you and discuss our goals and problems."

Zac, who was at the back, asked Bassy, who was sitting close to him, what the man's profession was.

"A lawyer. He didn't say it yet, but I know him," Bassy answered.

"And he's saying that he doesn't know what the government does with our tax money?" Zac asked.

"That's not what he said. Why can't we give him the opportunity to express himself well enough? He is still talking. It's too early to start judging." Before Bassy could caution Zac, people were clapping for Ed.

"Now, I missed that part because of you, Zac!"

"I have never been interested in politics," Ed continued, "but when things are going in the wrong direction, you should say, 'Enough is enough.' That is the essence of my coming out to fight for you."

"You're right!" someone screamed from the crowd.

"We can't fold our hands and expect the problems around us to solve themselves," Ed said. "It is not really possible for them to disappear on their own. I doubt it. If you do the same thing over and over again, you will get the same result over and over." The people applauded.

"He sounds like a good man" Lee said to the woman close to him.

"Yes. I think he is," she replied.

"Where has he been all these years when politicians were taking us for a ride?"

"Evidently, that's why he is coming out now," she answered him.

"He can play on the strings of people's hearts."

"Surely," she quickly added.

"Is he really running for—"

"Wait, let's hear him," the woman interrupted before he could ask his next question.

"I am here to get to know you," Ed said, "and we will know ourselves better very soon. As I said earlier, we need to send one of our own to the president's house at the capital—a powerful person who is willing and able to bring the type of changes for which you have been clamoring for a long time.

"You have been a wonderful audience. This is just the beginning of our getting together and the making of choices that will bring pride to all of us during the coming elections. Thanks to you all," he concluded.

There was loud applause.

Ed came down to shake hands and hug people. One woman told him that his speech was sentimental and made her cry.

"I'm glad you came," Ed told her. "I will be there for you and all the citizens of this country" We need to take our messages to the capital and all over the country, and I am here to do it for you. We have to take this country to another level,"

"I am happy that I didn't miss this," the woman said. "We were around here for a soccer game and were told that someone would be coming to this center to give a talk after the game. We chose to wait," she explained.

"Good idea," Ed complimented her.

"You want to be president of this country?" she asked.

"Yes. With your support, we can make it a reality."

"I think you've got all it takes."

"Thanks. I count on you, Ms. …?"

"Ms. Jen," she said.

"Thanks," Ed answered. "See you soon."

"You got it," She left, and the crowd gradually dispersed. Ed left with the friends who had come with him. Each one of them gave him a high five or a pat on the back.

"It wasn't bad," Ed said.

"Not at all," Willie quickly responded.

"You did a good job," Ola said.

"I hope the crowds continue like this," Bassy said.

TOWN HALL MEETING

"I am glad we pulled this one off. It wouldn't have been possible without each and every one of you," Ed said.

"It's not the time to compliment us," Zac replied. "We have an unwavering obligation to support you. That's what real friends are all about."

Their new friend Echi added that the egg had just been hatched and would grow on a day-by-day basis. He explained that they would be together until this endeavor was accomplished, no matter what it took.

"Today is a remarkable day," Onwa expressed, "mostly taking advantage of the soccer game that ended before our event. It helped to pull such a huge crowd. Again, Ed did a fabulous job, opening up his great mind and immense heart. I hope this opportunity will repeat itself from town to town and from coast to coast."

They all shook hands and promised to meet again at the Cultural Center for the next round. "If Ed continues with the energy he has acquired, nothing will stop him from taking this task against any person who comes to challenge him," Onwa explained.

Not far from the Cultural Center, a group of three people who had just left the town hall meeting were sitting at the nearby bus stop, expressing their opinions about Ed.

"He spoke well," Aku said.

"Oh yes, and like a politician," replied Carlos.

"He's not a politician, and he said it over there," Tylor clarified.

"What's his business again?" Carlos asked.

"A lawyer or something like that," Aku replied.

"A judge?" Taylor said.

"What's the difference? Most politicians are lawyers," Carlos said.

"I don't think so. There are a lot of businesspeople, and veterans too," Tylor replied.

"If they're not the same, they behave alike," Carlos said.

"What is he really running for? I didn't hear him say it," Aku said.

"Maybe for the Senate," Tylor said.

"He said he wants to go to the president's house at the capital, and also to take this country to another level," Carlos said.

"He can't be a president," Aku said. "He is just starting and has no experience. That office has a lot of responsibilities. You can't give it to a rookie."

"The interesting thing is that no one asked any questions," Carlos said. "What kind of town hall meeting is that, when no questions are asked?"

"He promised to come again," Tylor observed.

"It wasn't his fault that questions were not asked, though I saw people talking with him when he was walking around," Aku said.

As his bus pulled up to the stop, Carlos said, "Gentlemen, I have to leave. It has been a long day. I hope you all enjoy the rest of your day."

"Okay, gentlemen, I hope we meet again to continue with our conversations." Tylor walked away while Aku continued to wait for his own bus.

"Bye, everybody," Aku said.

When Ed got home, he was eager to share his experience at the town hall meeting with his wife and children. He thought such a successful story would persuade his wife to come on board. He believed that Titi's full participation would make a big difference, both morally and otherwise.

None of his family members were there when he got home, but he wasn't disappointed. He sat down cheerfully to relax before they got back. When he turned on the television to watch the evening news, the newscasters were talking about him. It was a big surprise because he didn't hadn't seen any media people there, and none had approached him. He believed one of the freelance journalists must have recorded the event, or a fan had sent information to the news media.

As he was still talking to himself, his wife, Titi walked in. "How was the meeting, darling?" she asked.

"It was spectacular. The hall was full and I was able to deliver my message."

"Congratulations on the first bold step. You are on your way to the capital, Your Excellency," she joked.

"Thanks, First Lady," Ed replied.

The children were also excited when they came back and their dad told them that the town hall meeting had been a big success. Everyone hoped the success of the meeting would be repeated at many other places.

Ed and his friends went back to the drawing table in preparations and arrangements for the second town hall meeting at the Cultural Center. Everyone was in high spirits. The expectation was for Ed to start declaring his candidacy more boldly at the meetings, and to keep emphasizing why he was running for the position. His friends wanted him to leave his mark any place he spoke to people, because he would not have the opportunity to meet the same people again.

Public talk had never been a problem for Ed as a lawyer, but in politics, the game was complicated. The political jury could quickly rule differently on your issues and give you the shock of your life. Running for public office required individuals with unusual ability and courage. The crowd that applauded you one day could boo you the next. That was why most distinguished men and women, and most virtuous citizens, stayed away from politics.

3

SECOND TOWN HALL MEETING

Ed was cheerful when he came to the Cultural Center. The hall was half full, unlike the first meeting, which had been crowded. Though it was a smaller in number, the audience seemed friendly. He was comfortable with them and expected to improve the publicity and the announcements, and also the sharing of fliers for future events. He did his best with the people who attended. In politics, you go with what you have at any particular moment.

He spoke eloquently and passionately. He was more precise on issues and accomplishments than he had been at the first meeting. People were quiet and nodding as he spoke. He was applauded several times, and once given a standing ovation.

There was no reason not to believe that Ed was learning well and fast. The first meeting had been a baby show compared with his vibrancy, the enthusiasm of the crowd, and his crafted skill in articulating his thoughts and reasoning. It would have been interesting to ask if he energized his crowd or his crowd energized him. Whichever way it worked, it was going well for him.

Ed aroused more appetite than he could feed. People wanted him to keep telling them what they wanted to hear, but he concluded his speech quickly so he could take questions. At the first meeting, he had spoken longer but hadn't taken questions. Instead he met people individually after his speech. This time, he made a short speech and wanted to take questions. He must have thought it would be a good idea, but he ended up being sucked up by it. It almost erased what he had achieved through his speech. Ed was grasping for answers to most of the important questions. An unanticipated reaction was triggered that left people questioning his knowledge of the problems in the towns and small communities, and his ability to deal with complicated issues when they arose.

Ed could have used the time of questions and answers to expatiate on his previously raised ideas and building more confidence in the minds of his listeners. He let the opportunity slip through his hands. It wasn't a surprise to the political veterans, because going into politics is like walking on slippery ground, expecting to tumble at any moment.

"You made an incredible speech," Eze began. "It's good to know if those of you who nurse the ambition to lead this country honestly and conscientiously understand our collective problems. I am saying this because most politicians prepare their speeches without having actual knowledge of the needs of the ordinary citizens in the little boroughs and towns. And my question is this: As a lawyer, have you ever given free service to any poor person in need?"

"Wonderful question!" Jesse said.

"Just perfect!" Su said

"What's your name again?" Ed asked.

"Eze."

"Thanks so much for your compliment," Ed began. "I have the honor to be here with you. The essence of this meeting today is for us to pull our resources together, figure out what we need as a community, and work together for the best interests of our country and its citizens."

"He has not answered the question," Mola whispered to Tiree, sitting close to her.

"That's exactly what they do—no direct answer," Tiree said. "I thought candidates coming up this year would show us something new and decent."

"Alex is raising his hand," Mola said.

"Ed's taking Isiah," Tiree said.

"Mr. Ed, have you heard about how autism spectrum disorder is devastating children in this country?" Isiah asked. "Have you contributed money or supported any causes to help these innocent citizens who are struggling to be like you and me?"

"It is something we would need to look into seriously. I have heard of it, but don't know much about it. You should be assured that I would work hard for everybody."

"I'm surprised you did not know about autism," Isiah replied. "In the next thirty to fifty years, half of this country will be autistic if proper action is not taken now."

"I didn't know it was that serious, but I agree with you," Ed replied.

"My name is Alex. I'm guessing that you have children. If you do, do they attend public or private schools?"

"You asked a beautiful question, Mr. Alex," Ed began. "If you listened well at the beginning of my speech, you know I have concerns about general problems that demand immediate government attention, both at the local and federal level. It is becoming more expensive to educate our children, and a lot of parents are having difficulty sending their children to school. That is one of the challenges demanding quick solutions. It is true that some government officials and those who can afford it send their children to private schools. A lot of factors contribute to that. It depends on the angle from which one looks at it. However, my priority would be to make sure every child in this country is properly educated."

More people were raising their hands, but it seemed that Ed was becoming uncomfortable with the barrage of questions. He thanked everybody for coming, waved to them, and left.

His departure didn't sit well with a lot of people. Many stayed behind, as if waiting for another speaker. Some of those who had asked questions, especially Alex, didn't think Ed had answered them effectively.

The questions from Isiah had hit Ed like lightning, and while he'd scrambled to find his feet, Alex had thrown in another punch as if to test his limit. He had been swallowed in a deep cloud of confusion and choking to get the right words out. Ed had managed to loosen up and take the next exit before he was embarrassed.

Ed left with his friends, though some of them didn't feel comfortable with the final outcome of the meeting. He had been unprepared for the questions that were thrown at him, and he started wondering if there would be the need to continue with the town meetings.

A handful of his friends were still optimistic and believed any damage done could be remedied, mostly because the campaign had not really shaped up yet.

"I think you did very well," said Onwa. "Your speech was marvelous and persuasive. I heard one man screaming, 'Yes! Yes!' It is good that some of these little issues are coming up now so that you'll be more prepared for the next event."

"There's no doubt that people ask all kinds of questions, both relevant and otherwise, during political events like this one," Zac said. "They want to know if their questions are understood, and whether their problems can be solved. The most important thing is to remain calm and prudent at all times."

Ed thanked his friends and asked to meet with them again to review strategies. All of them agreed to do so. He tried to be strong and avoid appearing frustrated at his own delivery, but his appearance betrayed him. He waved goodbye to them, and they dispersed.

Titi got home and found Ed slumped on the sofa like a fighter who had been knocked out in a boxing match. It seemed like his plans were crumbling, and he asked himself if he was making the right choices. He didn't want to give up yet, but was trying to think of a better way to move on.

"Get up, darling," she said. "Why are you so tired, and how was the event?" She was curious, although she may have been expecting to get the same answer she got after the first meeting.

"We started well. Everything went smoothly with some applause and a standing ovation," Ed explained. "I considered it a big success except the little hiccup we encountered at the end."

"What changed? Were there any fights or accidents?" she asked.

"No. Nothing like that," he said. "I started to take questions after the speech. Someone asked me if my children went to private or public schools. I felt ambushed, and didn't continue taking questions. My friends and I left."

"That's it?"

"Yes, honey."

Titi started laughing out loud.

"What's so funny?" he asked his wife. "You are making me feel stupid."

"No, darling. The prospective president of this country cannot be stupid," she quickly flattered him. "The tough part of it has not come yet. That will happen mostly when you get a challenger, unless you run unopposed."

"Run unopposed?" he asked. "But that has never happened in this country."

"Well, it has to happen before it becomes history, and it may happen one day," she said.

"I doubt it."

"Without mixing issues," she continued, "the importance of these exploratory meetings is for you to unfold some intricacies you will encounter at the higher level when you engage fully in the campaign. A lot of things will happen. People and the media will dig into your past and present, including your family means of livelihood."

"I know it, and my record is good," he said, taking a deep breath and sipping his water. "I told my friends that we would meet to review our position before arranging another town meeting, and they agreed."

"Sounds fine to me. You should also do it as early as possible, because in politics, time is of the essence," Titi said.

"You're right. I think I should make some quick calls now."

4

ED'S QUICK DEPARTURE

Ed had impressed his audience, but his speech was too short for people expecting him to convince them why he would be a better candidate than others. A lot of them didn't know why he suddenly stopped taking questions when many others were raising their hands. It was not clear whether he realized that his audience was expecting him to continue with his speech. Worst of all, he had taken few questions and given unsatisfactory answers before he left. Irrespective of all his shortcomings, Ed had won some fans, but he hadn't taken advantage of the situation. His premature departure created more problems than his responses to people's questions. Despite the vague answers, he had made some good points, and people were beginning to like him. A few others thought he was taking a short break and expected him to come back.

Alex, who realized the problem Ed had created, walked onto the stage as if he were one of the organizers, or trying to fill a vacuum. He seized the opportunity to advance his undeclared ambition, and exploited the advantage Ed hadn't used to impress his audience.

He began an impromptu speech: "Ladies and gentlemen, I didn't mean to come onto this stage this evening, but it seemed like most of you had not realized that our guest is gone. This is a political season, and we can see and hear a lot of things. I have no reason to doubt the genuineness of this gentleman and everything he said to us. However, his impression and expressions today didn't go deep enough to assure us that he fully understood our pains and pleasure. Personally, I did not understand whether he came to talk about his emotional desires to be president or to reason with us about the way we live our lives here. He could have been clearer about his ideas and ambitions, which could have helped us make a rational judgment about his preparedness to lead our country.

"As is the practice of people who seek to hold public offices, mostly the office of president, he should manifest his vision of reasons and his prospective contributions—qualitatively or quantitatively. Such causes and posterity would invigorate his listeners, helping them appreciate what he was saying and accept his imagination. Touching the right string of their sensation would make people's reasons run wild. If any person comes here and speaks haphazardly, we cannot follow blindly. He should answer our questions adequately and effectively, showing understanding of our concerns in the best possible way. We can still talk to ourselves; it's all about our communities. I have been a community person all my life. I have attended town hall meetings for all kinds of reasons—social or political, you name it."

Everyone was quiet as Alex unfolded his surprises. He continued with expressions that were touching them deeply. Ed's political dreams were gradually deflated, as he would find out soon.

"I don't know," Alex continued, "what each and every one of you derived from this meeting today. As for me, it ended when I thought it was picking up steam. It seemed that Ed was in a hurry, or was not fully prepared to talk to us and answer all our questions. He should have come at a better time rather than leaving us high and dry. We have better things to do than listen to a man who wants to pick and choose which questions to respond to, and with half answers too.

"I have no doubt in my mind that we are very vulnerable people, and that people often take advantage of us. But we are stronger and better than we demonstrate if we put our acts together. It is a fantasy that people would come here, sugarcoat their speeches, and expect us to vote for them when the time comes. We can do better than that, my people!"

"You are the man," Greg shouted from the back.

"It was your question that made Ed run away. Go ahead and talk to us," Uwa added.

"You're a very smart man," Terry said.

"And you hear it now and then that every disappointment from God is a blessing," Alex continued. "Let us use this opportunity to realign our thoughts and our commitments. We can produce the president of this country if we come together with one unbroken spirit. Let's be all we want to be."

"Yes. We're ready," Arch said.

"Let's get it done now," Lee said.

"We don't want anyone else; let it be Alex," Dobb said.

"And him only," Kele said.

"Ladies and gentlemen, we have spent a lot of time here today. Let us go home, and if you would accept my request, let's reassemble again, same time and same place next week, to continue with these issues," Alex said. "Let us seize this opportunity to discuss and fight our own fights. You have heard that the courage in the heart of a man is from either nature or habit. Whichever way, we cannot hide from ourselves. Spread the message so that more people will be here as scheduled. God bless."

There was loud applause.

"He is the best," Nkwa said.

"I was almost crying," Myria added.

"Let's all go home and come back next week," Stern said. "I will not miss one word from his speech next week."

When Alex was making his speech, it seemed like an opportunity he had been waiting for. He seized the moment and ran with it. It is said that the wind does not go through the same route twice in a lifetime. He had delivered a precise and explosive speech that left people intoxicated and ready for action. It stirred up a political tsunami waiting to consume unprepared and uninformed individuals stepping into the political arena. He surprised people with his eloquence and brazen display as a humble community person. As his message intensified, he stimulated their appetite to hear more about what they had missed from Ed.

If he had any prior political ambition, or was interested in other, bigger dreams, he must have concealed them in his mind. Having seen how people were reacting to his messages, he took the opportunity to exploit this event to his liking. All these developments were trapped in his heart and mind. His expression and body language manifested his intent to the people, exposing a seemingly innocent and unambitious person and his desire to exercise and build on his inspired performance. He went far enough to showcase himself, and inevitably aimed gradually at his target and hoped for the best.

5

THE RISE OF ALEX

It was only 4:00 p.m., and the town hall auditorium was already filled for the scheduled 5:00 p.m. event. Word about Alex's captivating speech spread like wildfire. Those who had heard Alex speak the first time didn't want to be late, and wanted to be in the front row. Many other people had been told about Alex and wanted to witness everything for themselves. It was spectacular how Alex became a celebrity because of Ed's involuntarily short speech and infamous early departure from the previous meeting.

Alex had been a community person and living a quiet life, but his works spoke volumes. Youths and young adults loved and respected him because of his involvement with them. He was a coach to most of them in various sports activities, and had encouraged and supported them at their different endeavors. Alex spent his money on them without asking for a refund. He was great orator who could easily persuade a school dropout to go back to school the next day. His priority had been to make the community children stay in school and perform at their best. He was the only parent some of these kids knew, a man with enormous patience and very religious. Alex never gave up on any child, even those who disappointed him. He was famous for quoting the saying that winners never quit and quitters never win, and had told the youths and young adults that the future of the country was in their hands. People close to him would tell you that he was driven by the love of bringing other people's potential to fruition.

The only thing people didn't know much about Alex was his politics. He didn't talk much about it and never campaigned for anyone. There was no doubt that he attended some of the town meetings and a few campaign rallies, but he was never directly involved. He encouraged people to vote at all times because it was the only means the citizens could use to express themselves clearly and loudly. People had heard him say that democracy was the best system of government that human beings had invented, despite being abused by some people. He did not hide his feeling that power belonged to the people.

It was a surprise to many people when they heard Alex was having a rally at the Cultural Center. Some said it was a political rally, others said it was social. Whichever one, Alex was not known for rallies. He was a gentle man who knocked at people's doors, holding his fliers when he needed some support for activities he was having for youths or young adults, whom he called his kids.

This was a new Alex with a new agenda. Whatever he wanted to tell the people, they were ready to listen. He was deeply overwhelmed when he saw the crowd waiting for him. Something that had started with a small crowd had turned into a multitude.

He came out at exactly 5:00 p.m., and there was a standing ovation for him. Waving cheerfully in his decently tailored summer attire, he begged people to sit down.

"Thank you," he started.

There was loud applause.

"Thank you! Thank you!"

More applause.

"I am greatly—"

He was interrupted by applause.

"I am greatly flattered by this celebrity reception. I thought this was going to be a simple meeting like the last one, to talk about ourselves and our communities and to prepare for the selection of a new president. The coming election is important to us because we didn't benefit much from the current president despite all our support of him. Some of you must have seen or met some individuals hovering around our neighborhoods recently, talking about the coming election. Where have these people been all these years?"

There was much applause and laughter.

"In fact, this election is the epitome of our gathering this evening.

Enough is enough. The behavior of some of these so-called politicians is beginning to trouble me as a person. I don't know about you all. I am spiritually and emotionally fragmented, and you should feel the same way, because we are linked together in our causes and needs. I could not sleep all night, especially, remembering how my people of this community and environs had always been treated. I am thinking how I could make each and every one of you feel the same way I feel about this community and about our nation. These politicians come to us here and go to other communities to blow their trumpets, and when they depart, we are left with porous promises. If you looked closely at their behaviors, despite their rhetoric to conquer our spirits, you would quickly notice the disconnect. Obviously, there's no cordial connection between them and we the people. Any of them who is interested in being the president of this country shouldn't start campaigning by merely taking bold steps, or because they can speak well. You shouldn't run for office because you have the chance or the constitutional right to do so; there must be a true purpose and a goal. You should have this nation passionately in your heart and mind, with a genuine and authentic desire."

The audience clapped loudly.

"Poor Alex. He has us in his heart," Don said.

"He is illustrious," Bia responded.

"Alex the Great," Ham said.

"We will follow him and do everything he asked us to do," Scott vowed.

"Let's hear him talk. He has started again," Sam requested.

"Please, let's hear him again," Scott said.

"Let us use this moment, season, and occasion to awake from our slumbers," Alex asserted. "Let's tell the people coming to us the ways we think and feel. Left alone, I would want us to organize ourselves, and take our messages to the capital so that the president we elected into office would hear us from his open doors and windows. If you're disillusioned or feeling sour as our democracy is corrosively diminishing, this is the time to take initiative. We have to take this message to them and not wait until they come down here to shake our hands, kiss our babies, and make false promises. Both those in government now and the few we have seen showing interest in replacing them don't seem to have any short- or long-term goodwill for you and me."

The applause lasted a long time.

"This man speaks my mind," Shola said.

"A wonderful person," Jose added.

"Better than all the politicians," Myria said.

"I'm going to the capital with him," Abu said.

"Me too," Jose said.

"We are all going," Don said.

"Wait, he's not finished," Sam said.

"As we all know, the only thing that is constant is change," Ed said. "We have been fighting for our communities at different levels, but our leaders adopted inadequate means and ways of treating our concerns. I know all of you are disgusted with the decay of the time. You are all yearning for a prosperous tomorrow, a daunting task to survive the present challenging lifestyle. Virtually every citizen should be carried along to worthy ends, but the unpleasant reality is that their greed and their overambition triumphed over their reason and humanity. If they could realize that everything that comes to life must die and decay, they would not subject the disadvantaged to undue hardships, but help them to meet their needs. Ladies and gentlemen, there is the saying that where your treasure is, your heart is also. Failure is not our portion, because we don't deserve it."

The applause was long and loud.

"A piece of cake is no more enough for us. Our experiences are now shaping our grievances and demands. When—"

He was interrupted by applause.

"When citizens are treated the way they don't deserve, there are bound to be disappointments, frustration, and anger," Alex said. "We can't be silent anymore. Otherwise our silence would mean that we would die quietly and disappear. Things do not get better by being left alone. We are people of the same hopes and dreams. By all the exigencies of a practical life, unpopularity is earned by dishonorable actions. My people, we cannot hide the realities from ourselves again."

"Never and ever," Don said.

"We will fight for our communities," Umar said.

"We will go to the capital and tell them our minds," Pete declared.

"Tell the people in other communities to go with us. We'll scream and shout until the president and all the politicians listen to us, or be gone," Cliff said.

"My people and fellow citizens," Alex continued.

"Silence. Let's hear from our future leader," Pete said.

"Our contemporary leader," Don added.

"The true man of the people," Abu said.

"He's talking—let's hear him!" Jose said.

"Let me not take too much of this evening," he continued. "Can we all converge at the Capital National Park three weeks from today, by one p.m.?" he asked.

The crowd roared, "Yeeessss"

"Can you tell your friends, community members, and relatives all over the nation to join us for this common cause?"

"Yes," they responded.

"I want you all to go in peace and prepare for this wonderful trip to the Capital National Park coming soon. This is the beginning of our journey to fight the unjust policies we have tolerated for too long. It is the time to tell the people we voted into office that they are not genuinely concerned about us and do not feel the pains of the ordinary citizens. Since none of them is fighting for us, we're ready to lead our own fight. The behaviors of these people at the capital are unrealistic and unacceptable. What seemed like constraints and bad dreams, and unattainable fairyland, would change to prevailing victory and affections," Alex stated.

"Go ahead and speak for us," Ikye said.

"We are here today to raise not money, but hope for ourselves and our children. Our youths and young adults should have confidence in this nation and appreciating what it meant to be a citizen of this nation. Our most profound gift to our high school and university graduates would be to replace their unemployment with jobs, and to replace illusions with hopes and fulfillment. It is not a privilege but a right to have a government that shares our pains and demonstrates understanding of our common good, giving our children the dignity and ability to live their dreams."

"I was consumed by the power of his speech, almost crying," Adam confessed.

"I don't think any good citizen would want to miss this trip in the next few weeks," Papi said. "Nobody has seen anything like this in this century. We have to believe in ourselves and change our mind-set. Everyone has to be part of this movement because the future coming to us cannot be better unless it enhances what we have."

"I will surely be there, God willing," Ije said. "What could be more beautiful than fighting for a good cause?"

"Let's go home, everybody, and spread the news," Don said.

"All of us will move boldly to the capital city," Papi said.

There were some others who didn't say anything, but it was easily noticed that they were emotional. A few of them came out of the meeting and were yet undecided, though concerned about the community issues which they wanted to separate from political undertones. Although not to everybody Alex seemed again to be a hidden angel who would uplift them without any fear or favor. His marvelous performance threw challenges to people both present and absent to be involved in the new movement. Going to Capital National Park became the best channel to make their voices heard. It was not a tested process but sounded like a noble idea, especially coming from such a new hero with such a persuasive voice.

Most of the people didn't want to miss the opportunity to witness the event, even those who weren't quite sure how they would benefit from it. Alex had been seen as a brave and bright man who showed that he had a big heart. His clever assessments and brave speech carried all the small towns around, creating a sudden fame that would need hard work to maintain.

The indisputable challenge to Alex and the other supporters was the mobilizing of people nationwide, and how they would go to Capital National Park. Many individuals would need to go from city to city and town to town, notifying people and confirming that large numbers of people and vehicles would go to Capital National Park for the historic gathering.

The fastest thing on this planet is news. It could spread through tested and untested, natural and supernatural mechanisms. The story about Alex was all over the place and spreading even faster.

Alex went home, astonished by the compelling response and reaction he was getting. He asked himself if this was a calling or something else. Consumed in diverse thoughts, he sat sedately on the sofa in his living room and looked through the windows. The breeze was blowing quietly and the trees and grasses were bending their heads. He had an involuntary feeling about how the invisible wind was courteously and triumphantly respected when passing by.

"What a nice breeze!" he said to himself.

He was overwhelmed with emotion as he tried to fashion out how he would help himself. It was a wake-up call, and he had never been in politics at this level before, with its overwhelming commitment. He had created a big impression of himself, and as a consequence, people had huge expectations of him. It was why it was said that to whom much is given much is expected.

Alex made some calls to a few of his friends, expecting to get some soothing advice. Most of them told him to take his best performance to National Park, where he would be expected to make or break his campaign. It was an overwhelming feeling, and he started getting worried and noticeably shivering. His blood was speeding from his head down to his feet and up again. He was being tortured by his imagination and pretensions. As he was reflecting on the challenges ahead of him, he jumped up from the sofa and went to take a cold shower.

The cold shower gave him an unmatched relief, calming his boiling nerves, and he was able to sit down again to navigate through the terrain and landscape of his clustered feelings, gradually making a directional headway.

Alex knew he had surprised himself and his friends. He had never expected to inflame people's sentiments to such a sudden and explosive level, which eventually energized them to consider going to the national capital. Nobody was complaining about anything about him; on the contrary, he was seen as a messiah who had come to remove the barrier that demarcated and degraded the populace from privileged politicians. Again, he did not present himself as anyone other than an ordinary community man, as was expected of him. Though he did not specifically declare his purpose, his thoughts, expressions, and the targeted concerns revealed that he wanted to be president. He agreed with the public opinion about the unparalleled need to select new leadership.

While he was trying to enjoy his privacy, his doorbell rang. He was surprised, because he was not expecting anyone. Reluctantly getting up and peeping through the peephole in the door, he saw that it was his best friend, DJ.

"What are you doing here?" he asked jokingly, and opened the door.

DJ laughed loudly while hugging him.

"You didn't tell me you were coming," Alex said.

"I really wanted to go home but was propelled by your speech to come down here."

"That's funny," Alex responded. "How was my speech?"

"It was extremely effective and extraordinarily successful. You could tell by the way people were applauding you that everything was spectacular," DJ said.

"Thank you for the nice observation," Alex replied. "I was sincerely pouring out the things that had been on my mind for a long time. You know I am not a campaigner, but suddenly, this intuition overtook me."

"Intuition to be the president?" DJ asked.

"If the citizens of this great nation want me to be their president, I cannot say no to them." Both of them laughed, and they gave each other a high five.

Alex said on a serious note that every success comes with a price. He added that his head was getting heavy with thoughts about how to get himself ready for the big day at National Park.

"There is no doubt that it will be the only day in your life, the only opportunity to show the world whether you are speaking from your heart or your mouth," DJ explained to him. "You have to express yourself sincerely for people to believe you. People have seen great leadership in you as you continue to manifest a clever assessment of the country's problems."

"I will try my utmost best," Alex said. "With all the celestial blessings, I will galvanize my audience. People who are coming to the capital will be energized and enlightened. That's my expectation for that day."

"I will be there by the will of our Lord God," DJ said.

"I know you will be there, DJ," Alex replied. "You must have forgotten that it was you who put this thing into my head."

"How and when?" DJ asked.

"The day you visited me at the community center. I was with some young adults who had dropped out of school. When we came out, you said that I was sitting on a diamond mine, that I had the potential to rule this country. I didn't really comprehend what you meant, but it had been in my mind. Working with youths and young adults was not a high-paying job, I said to myself then, but I wondered what it had to do with ruling this country. Now it seems like a prophecy."

"Oh! Okay! Now I remember. I knew you were not excited about politics. Neither were you a public speaker. I saw how you could easily persuade some of those difficult young adults, making them exercise self-control in the community to avoid getting into trouble. They listened to you, and some of them went back to school or entered technical institutions. I knew you could use that talent in a broader way. Any person who can solve the problems of those young men and women can easily lead this country. I am glad you have proven me right."

"I appreciate that confidence, DJ."

After brainstorming for a few minutes, DJ left to allow Alex to get to work toward the rally at Capital National Park.

As Alex closed his door, he prayed and began to reflect on everything he had been told. He was a little nervous going to speak to such an enormous crowd, but he softly said to himself, "I will make sure I give the nation an honorable and triumphant speech to remember for a long time."

He began to prepare the speech for the Capital National Park rally. It was obvious to him that it would be a formidable opportunity to discover how he would be evaluated in the public's eyes and minds. The citizens would find out he could be trusted with their future, and their children's and grandchildren's future, or they would dump him and describe him as a mere town crier or clown.

6

ED'S NEW CHALLENGES

Ed met with his friends to discuss the new developments and how to neutralize them. The most shocking of all to him was how Alex had come up from nowhere to dominate the whole political climate. It was hard to classify Alex's initial move as anything serious because he could not be classified as a political candidate or an activist. He had come out of the blue to be relevant. Just like in this country, which was different from every other, he had the freedom to express his feelings as he wanted, and could do it without any boundaries. There was nothing extraordinary about it.

"The great concern, however," Ed said to his friends, "is Alex's sudden fame and popularity, which are blowing like a hurricane. It looks frightful that no one wants to get in his way. What are we going to do now? This is a serious threat to everything we have been trying to accomplish. Do we give up or challenge him vigorously?"

"I don't think his position has a clear definition," Chief said. "I was blown away by what I heard about him. He was practically unknown before he attended the community town hall meeting, but now he's spreading like a raging wildfire. We need to know what he is promising the people, so that we could realign our logistics."

"My understanding is that he's astonishing people with his rhetoric, almost holding prospective candidates in bondage because they have not figured out how to neutralize or measure equally with him," Ade said. "He has broken all the historical rules of the political processes. The political parties are muted and cannot act, and the independents have lost the strength of their mind. Unfortunately or fortunately for him, his behavior is being rewarded for excellence by the public without much scrutiny. People have made swift changes because of the man they say has unrivaled talent.

"My opinion, judging from the new developments, is to slow down; this seems to be a bad season for politics. Alex has dampened people's minds about politicians and put enormous responsibilities on the shoulders of those who might want to run for any office. His group has galvanized a great number of people from all over the nation to go to the capital for a rally. And they have done it on short notice."

"It sounds crazy to me," Ed remarked. "Alex seemed like one of the people who asked questions at the Cultural Center town hall meeting."

"Yes, he was," Cole said. "For whatever reasons, he took advantage of your departure to make a speech to the same audience. They met again at the same venue, and people started liking him. People are listening to him and believing his message. I heard he is very persuasive, with ineradicable peace-loving and intellectual tones."

"What was his message?" Tom asked.

"I heard he was talking about the uncertainty of the economy, education, and the disaffection this nation is going through, and he placed the blame on the politicians who ignored the hopes and fears of their constituencies while acquiring stupendous wealth for themselves," Jesse said. "He was talking about trust and honesty in dealing with the citizens, and arousing the emotions on the issue that politicians are practicing extreme inequalities in the country. He also painted politicians as those who always forget their electorates until election time, when they return with sugarcoated promises that are never translated into action."

"The rally at Capital National Park will be a challenging test for him," Ade said. "His impression on local supporters could be different from how people perceive him nationally. If he fails to deliver compelling messages at the rally, it will be his end, and the door will be wide open for others. If he makes a successful rally, it will complicate what we're trying to do. Pulling a large crowd at National Park and convincing them of his agenda would be difficult to overcome, especially for a new and unpopular candidate. I heard he said that politicians and diapers have one thing in common: they should both be changed regularly and for the same reason. Competing with him as it is now, or after a successful rally, would be like standing in front of a moving train. Whether right or wrong, it sounds like he will bring down any person competing with him."

"It's frustrating how a rat grew overnight to become an elephant," Ed said. "However, he hasn't done anything extraordinary other than get a few steps ahead of us. It's like he hacked my agenda and ran away with it. Do we all agree to wait until the rally at National Park is done? And, who really is this Alex?" Ed was frustrated.

"He is a hero among the youths and young adults," Noah said. "He coached some of them in different sports activities, and never left behind anyone who came to him. Some of the youths who dropped out of school were redirected and counseled to return to school. He built strength and hope in them and helped them see the light at the end of the tunnel. A lot of these kids benefited from his guardianship and mentorship. He never ran for office and never showed any interest in politics, but if he contested this election today, all the young adults would vote for Uncle Alex, as they popularly call him."

"I think he has a wonderful résumé, but there is no indication that he wanted to run for the presidency," Noah said. "Why shouldn't he run for other positions? He looks like a mere community activist. We need to know if he is shifting his position and transforming it into something else. There are good chances of working with him and steering him to a different position. He could be promised a particular position. We can understand his zeal now, but when a seed germinates, it does not get green until it sees the light. On the contrary, he must have waited for this opportunity without telling anybody—staying calm like a dormant volcano."

"As it was rightly said earlier, the only thing that could minimize this panic is if Alex failed to galvanize both the middle class and the lower class at the rally," Chief said. "We would move in forcefully and aggressively to slow him down and treat him like a messenger who could not be the master. Remember, we are talking about the president of this powerful country. There is a genuine and diligent way to sidetrack whatever he is doing and come up with a new, flourishing idea; timing is everything. People seem to be happy with him now, but happiness is as temporary as sadness is. Neither of them last forever. The next line of action is to find out if any of us will be going to the rally at National Park so we can get an eyewitness account. It would be fantastic if any or some of us could make it. The news is everywhere, and a lot of people are curious about him."

Ed looked expressionless and confused while expecting his friends to say something more encouraging. The room was exceptionally quiet, as if the group had run out of ideas. Everyone seemed to be looking at each other to make a contribution. The expectant feeling between them drifted sluggishly, and Ed suddenly gave a dry laugh, like a person feeling empty and meaninglessness.

As if to jump-start the conversation, he said, "Waiting for this Capital National Park rally is like mental torture. One day looks like a week, and one week looks like a month—an endless and miserable problem. I would have preferred that we had other, varied strategies to chew on while other events develop. It wouldn't be a bad idea having another town hall meeting somewhere before the rally, trying to counter the impression that Alex has a celestial solution to the national problems."

"This wait and see is the best option we have now," Bassy said. "We are momentarily in a chain, and the most prudent choice is to wait for the appropriate time to make a new move. If we take the wrong action, it will feed the interest and ambition of our adversary. The indisputable truth is that Alex is passionately capitalizing on the attention he is getting now, and if the uncertainty of matching up his popularity outweighs our present tactics, we would have to make an authentic and painstaking decision." Bassy paused as if weighing his thoughts.

"The courage and desires may be there," he continued, "but we have to avoid disaster when it is obvious. This is a game of numbers. The result may not change even when one appears at the public place on the scaffold to enumerate a million things to do for the people. It is obvious that a lot of citizens feel that this government has failed them, and they want a new beginning. We don't know if this new beginner will be Ed, Alex, or someone else yet to come out. Very soon, we will know if Ed needs to nourish his dream of being president or take a pause," Bassy concluded.

After all the discussion and no one volunteering to attend the rally at National Park, Ed went home worried. He believed that the most authentic story should be from an eyewitness. But Ayo, one of the associates, went home and thought deeply about the rally. He accepted within himself that it would be a reward and a tangible remedy for Ed's strategic planning if one of them made the sacrifice to be at National Park to evaluate the rally. He decided to attend without telling Ed or any of his other friends. Everything about Alex and this rally was developing fast, and in defiance against all odds.

"My going to this rally will bring sanity and security to our group," Ayo said to himself. "It will also offer a creative solution, because I will bring undiluted information from there. Considering real choices and making decisions from them, rather than depending on hearsay, will be crucial. We will not do ourselves any favors by chasing imaginary sentiments. This particularized and popularized rally could be a tigress that was pregnant and delivered a mouse, and I want to be proved wrong."

7

TORTOISE AND THE SQUIRREL

When Ed experienced difficult and emotional moments, he had three ways to deal with them that he considered therapeutic. One, he would go out with his children to the park to play tennis or basketball. Two, he would stay home to cook, mostly when his wife was not at home. He enjoyed cooking. His youngest son liked to stay around him any time he was cooking, especially because it meant he would be the first to taste his dad's food. Finally, Ed loved telling his children stories, both stories from real life and folktales. His youngest son believed his dad would narrate wonderful animal stories while he was cooking.

The most remarkable tale his dad narrated, according to the boy, was about a tortoise and a squirrel. His dad told him why the tortoise had a broken back and walked like a very old man. And the story, according to the boy, who retold it, was about a famine in the animal kingdom.

"There was a famine in the animal kingdom," Ed's young son said. "It started when there was no rain for a long time and all the plants and vegetables were dying. The rivers and lakes were drying up. All the animals were starving. The little food available was given to the Lion King, elephants, and other big animals. Other, little animals were starving to death.

"One day, the Lion King summoned all the animals for a general meeting to discuss the famine and how to survive it. Any animal who failed to show up, he said, would be killed. All of them assembled at the King's Square on the day and time that was scheduled.

THE KING

"After listening to the different opinions of the animals, the Lion King was not satisfied. The tortoise suggested that birds be sent to a distant land to buy food. The Lion King didn't think it was a good idea. Finally, he mandated that the animals reduce the population of the kingdom so that there would be enough food for the living animals. All the animals were given two weeks to kill their mothers. The king's mother was exempted.

"This information was awful to the animals. There were a lot of cries, and the king ordered all of them to disperse. He scheduled another meeting within two weeks for everybody to convene again so he could find out who didn't obey the order. It was a terrible day in the animal kingdom.

"The squirrel went home and started thinking about what to do. He loved his mother very much and didn't want to kill her. He came up with a smart idea to hide his mother at the top of the mountain where no animal would find her. The first step was to go every night to the land of the humans to gather food that would sustain his mother for a long time at the mountain.

"After one week, the squirrel took his mother to the mountain. Everything was a bonded secret between him and his mother. He scheduled times he would be visiting her. All the arrangements worked out perfectly well."

THE MOUNTAIN

"As time went by, the king's plan to reduce the population as a means of controlling the famine wasn't working. All the animals killed their mothers, but it didn't solve anything. Starvation was worsening, and the animals were losing weight every day.

"The tortoise was surprised that the squirrel was always looking good while other animals were drying up. One day, the tortoise went to the squirrel and begged to be his friend. After a short while, he wanted to know the secret of how the squirrel was keeping himself healthy. The squirrel didn't want to tell him. After several days of the tortoise begging and pleading, swearing not to tell any other animal, the squirrel changed his mind. He scheduled a trip with the tortoise to see his mother.

"On that special day, the squirrel took the tortoise to the valley of the mountain. He began to sing to his mother while the tortoise listened attentively. When his mother heard his son's voice, she threw down the rope she kept for her son to climb up to the top. The squirrel climbed to the top with the tortoise. His mother didn't like seeing the tortoise because he was a sneaky animal. She knew it was too late and pointless to complain about her son's mistake. The damage had been done. She attended well to all of them. The tortoise seemed to be happy and thanked her for her hospitality. The squirrel and his friend came down from the mountain.

"As the tortoise was going home, he could not believe an animal like the squirrel could outsmart all the animals. However, he was happy to have discovered the secret. He started planning to go back to the mountain to ask for food from the squirrel's mother any day he was hungry. He promised himself he would reveal the secret if she refused to attend to him again.

"One day, tortoise was very hungry. He prepared to return to the mountain. He didn't inform his new friend, the squirrel. He went to the valley of the mountain as his friend had taken him, and began to sing like the squirrel had. Believing it was her son, the squirrel's mother threw down the rope, expecting her son to climb up. Unfortunately for the tortoise, the squirrel was visiting his mother the same day and at the same time. He reached the valley and got the shock of his life. He discovered what the tortoise had done, and sang back to his mother to cut the rope immediately. By then, the tortoise was halfway to the top. The squirrel's mother cut the rope and the tortoise fell hard on the ground. He did not die, but he broke his back and sustained a lot of injuries."

Engaging with family activities or interacting with his children was the most genuine avenue Ed used to escape real or artificial distress coming his way. Ed's last son could not understand how his dad knew all his stories. One thing was certain: he had always enjoyed every one of them. The squirrel story sounded magical to him, and the squirrel's cleverness at hiding his mother was amazing. The only sad part was the revealing of his mother's secret to the tortoise.

Ed was proud of the time he spent with his family. It was a big pause from political activities and an opportunity, especially at this particular time, to study how Alex's movement was developing. One surprising observation from his youngest son that made everybody laugh was when he asked his dad if he would still cook for them if he won the election. Ed jokingly told him that the family routines would not change, including everybody doing their chores in the house.

8

CAPITAL NATIONAL PARK RALLY

The feelings at National Park were heating up like an uncontrollable wildfire. The people who organized the event were enthusiastic, and some attendants, mostly those who hadn't attended the town hall meeting, were curious to hear Alex make his speech. It was a highly charged arena, as though the crowd was waiting for the returning of war heroes. Some people came with the national flag, and others were singing the national anthem. The experience was unprecedented, mostly for an individual virtually unknown nationwide to attract such a crowd. All kinds of people were there, from youths to young adults to old men and women.

As all the people were still waiting for Alex to come out, some curious individuals who didn't know him were asking around to get more information about him and his agenda. The news about the rally went around fast like a jet, and many people didn't have time to ask questions about the gathering.

"Who is this man we are waiting for?" Ami asked his friend.

"I don't really know him, but people are saying very good things about him," Uwa said. "I am here out of curiosity to know what he's up to. I don't want to miss this rally, which was well publicized. I wouldn't want other people to tell me about it."

"Is he running to be the next president?" Ami asked.

"His message seemed mixed," Uwa replied. "To my understanding, he has not declared wholly and openly if he is running for any particular office, unless he declares today. Personally, I would not regard this as a political rally," he added.

"We are already here. Let's see what he has for us," Ami said.

"You are perfectly right. I wouldn't want people to tell me what happened. That's why I come here to witness it myself."

There were cheers and loud applause as Alex started for the podium.

"What's this applause for?" Boxer asked.

"I think Alex is coming up to the podium," Kele responded.

"Can we all see him?" Boxer asked.

"I hope the park podium is high enough for us to see him from this corner," Kele said.

The applause intensified as Alex got closer.

"Yes, he's here now. I can see him," Boxer said.

"He is waving to people," Nick explained.

"Thank you! Thank you! Thank you!" Alex greeted.

"Wait, everyone. He is talking," Nick said.

"Fellow citizens and friends," Alex started, "let me thank you all for coming from far and near to embrace this moment. I am greatly honored to be here with you. I know each one of you has important things to do today, but you chose to be here. You should be well assured that your presence here will change the history of this, our beloved country. I haven't an infinitesimal doubt in my mind and heart that you will leave here more prepared, more knowledgeable, and more convinced about the direction in which you think our nation is drifting. It is a monumental honor standing at this platform and speaking to this noble audience."

"Alex! Alex! Alex!" the crowd shouted.

"Let me start my speech today by talking about the debilitating democracy we are experiencing in our own time. We should know the problem of leadership in this country, followed by the behavior of our elected politicians we voted into office to protect our interests. Those in government offices and the corridors of power should understand the people's feelings, disillusionment or disappointment. They should be there for the good of their people and humanity.

"The president is of the utmost importance to me because he is in the driver's seat of the affairs of this nation. I will talk more about his leadership. He is the one who navigates our affairs when challenges drift to all kinds of directions, both from the expected and the unexpected.

"Let me tell you a quick story of a woman I met just yesterday. She has three young children and two jobs, and is always running from one job to the other. Her husband died a year ago because of hardship and poor health care in this country. She asked why our dreams are out of reach despite all the citizens' hard work and good efforts.

"She's not the only citizen who has asked such a question. Most of us in distress and despair have asked many times, 'What's wrong with our country?' You and I have been in constant toil, waiting for our dreams to come through; dreams cannot be fulfilled and citizens are struggling in a rich country to provide for their own needs. These conditions bruise the nation's pride. We have hibernated enough. It is true that government is a stage, and I think the people running our government now should allow other actors to play their parts. Let's get out of our shells and use our God-given courage to prevail against our fears."

There was loud applause.

"The ship of our nation," Alex continued, "is being tossed around by an artificial storm created by our leaders. It is evident, good, and wise that what we will achieve by coming together today would influence the force and method to bring success, happiness, and well-being for ourselves, our children, and our grandchildren. Our coming here is torture, because we didn't need to travel this far to the capital under this scorching sun to explain ourselves and to be heard. When life is provisional, no one can plan for the future. However, we should always learn from our ancestors, who went down the roads we are traveling now, and benefit from their experiences, which are inspirational. From the sovereignty of reason, we can never allow this immeasurable values bequeathed to us to be ruined. *'Per crucem ad lucem*—from the sacrifice flashes forth the light.'"

The applause was loud.

"Speak on, Alex. We are listening," Don said.

"He is our man," Kele said.

RALLY

"Quiet, my friends. He's still talking," Boxer said.

"I am a citizen of this beautiful country, born and raised here, and always ready to die for it. I am a war veteran, having used my sweat and blood to defend my country. That's how proud I am of it," Alex said boldly.

More clapping followed.

"I will tell you what I think about this, our beloved country, and I know you will agree with me because it concerns you. We need a new spirit and a new direction. We need to discover our nation and restore confidence in our system."

"Yes! Yes! Yes!" the crowd exploded. "Alex! Alex! Alex!"

"This is a legitimate voice," Kele said.

"He's making a beautiful speech," Boxer said admiringly.

"Very convincing," Uwa said.

"He is a visionary," Ami said.

"This country needs to be transformed, and it is high time the voices of the people are heard. Do you all love this country?" Alex asked.

"Yeaaaaah!" the crowd roared.

"So do I. It is incredibly certain that each and every one of us came here today for the better glory of this nation. Sure, that's why we are here. We must take positive actions to salvage it. We are the people, and we have the potential to inject new life into the things that hold us together—the country we hold dear." Alex waved his hands as he spoke. "We are people of the same hope and dream."

The applause lasted a long time.

"This is the most wonderful time for us to be here and speak our minds. Speech is very important, and the wisest people on earth use it most. Let our speech not only express our love, patriotism, and enthusiasm, but also contain them. Let's continue to renew our confidence, knowing there's something hopeful to live for."

People clapped again.

"We shall make him a senator!" Boxer said.

"No. President!" Kele said.

"Let him be the president," Nick added.

"Yes, he is equal to the task," Kele said.

"Vote for him and no one else," Don said.

"Again and again and again," Papi said.

"He will rule us for life," Mia said.

"He has a good heart, and is almost crying at the podium," Kele noticed.

"Humble, passionate, and vibrant," Uwa said.

"He's the only individual who understands the problems of this country," Dobb said.

"He would make us number one again," Brian said.

"He shall live long, and shall rule this country," Collin said.

"There's no—" Alex continued.

"Silence—he is not finished," Uwa interrupted.

"There is no better time than now to redirect our destiny to reflect our true values," Alex maintained. "This is the time to send a strong message of strength and resolve. If you lack the courage and the willingness to take your future into your own hands, to show the ability to confront the needs of this contemporaneous time, there will not be any tangible remedy at sight. We should all rise together and put our energies and passion together, and show force and gallantry. We must show willpower or the pursuit of it. With noble creation and growth, this is a nation of extensive wealth in everything, both real and imaginary."

The applause was loud and long.

"This gathering is the manifestation of the will of the people, an expression of hope and determination to rebuild and restructure our desires so we can give our citizens the opportunity to live up to their highest potential. This is the time to provide a future for our youths and young adults, to encourage growth and development for our nation to prosper. If things are allowed to continue the way they are, it will be like a fire lit now to burn us and future generations. We cannot allow our future to be blurred or our expectations to go with the wind."

There was more applause.

"The best asset for this nation is to have an admirable leader with reputable behavior and moral decency. We want an individual with lasting integrity and an articulated vision. It would be a stimulant and enticement for the young ones, and an ultimate triumph for the old. They are not hard to find, because we have the finest and noblest people in the world."

Loud applause erupted like a volcano.

"A-lex! A-lex! A-lex!" filled the air.

"He is spectacular," Brian said.

"He makes a wonderful speech and carries everyone with him," Onu added.

"A genuine president," Brian said.

"Our president without any doubt!" Eze said.

"I feel like I'm meditating," Shola said.

"A maverick," Ade said.

"Brilliant," Onu said.

"He has a pious heart," Uwa said.

"A man of sharp and speedy intellect," Ade added.

"The most loved man in this country," Eze said.

"A man with the most unfailing integrity," Shola said.

"He is very smart," Uwa said.

"Yes, a man of substance," Eze said.

"The most qualified to lead this country," Don affirmed.

"This is the advent of a new era," Bill said.

"He has won my affection," Liz said.

"The best," Uwa said.

"He will be the greatest president ever," Eze said.

"I will knock on every door to get all the votes, and everyone with a good conscience will vote for him," Ade said.

"Wait: he has not said he wants to be president," Bill said.

"We don't want anyone else," Uwa said.

"This is truly the man who would make this nation the greatest of all nations," Liz said.

SUPPORTERS

"I hope he wouldn't change like the others if he gets the position," Bill said.

"Never and ever," Uwa responded. "He has this country in his heart and would bring smiles to all of us again."

"He is the voice of wisdom," Don said.

"Really, really wonderful," Shola added.

"What we are …"

"Wait, people! Alex is talking," Brian said.

"Absolute silence! I want to hear every word he says," Uwa said.

"What we are doing now, I think, is refusing to give up," Alex said.

"Forward ever!" Ade said.

"I may be sounding emotional, so pardon me," said Alex, "but I look at the magnitude of this crowd and have deep insight into your individual expectations for what this country is meant to be. I understand the reasons why you expect more from the people you supposedly entrusted with your hopes and dreams, but they continue to fail you in all their dispensations. I could not help but get emotional. During my quiet moments, I put on my thinking cap and asked myself how long this great nation would continue to endure unnecessary political and social exploitation. This generation has a lot of unanswered questions, and if we don't react now, we will dwell on this terrifying symbol of our time."

The crowd applauded.

"The most indefensible aspect of it all is the failure to take action to control the outrageous crimes and related deaths in our communities. The neighborhoods that used to be peaceful and tranquil are going down at an alarming rate. Beyond the reach of time and change, someone has to offer sanity against madness. The worst travesty of all is the marginalization and neglect of the masses by the individuals whose only interest is to rape our treasury. My fear has been that if nothing is done, it will be impoverishing and tremendously evil for our children and grandchildren.

"Looking deeply into your hearts and minds, I could feel your great anger and sorrow. I am feeling with you as you ask for something new. We should not allow the things that brought small communities down to eat deeply into the fabric of this nation. It's incumbent on us to display our patriotic sentiments now or stay quiet forever. Let's face this task with sustained efforts for the good of our country and humanity. This is a battlefield we should not leave in anger. Otherwise it will breed more violence."

The crowd applauded.

"In times of danger, you must be courageous enough to stand for your country," Alex continued. "We have a wealth of opportunities to make good choices, and at this time of uncertainty, this moment of need, we must allocate our choices to the person who understands this nation's core values. If our political system is developing or has developed cracks, as it seems it has, we have to patch or rebuild it to prevent being consumed by the deterioration."

There was lengthy applause.

"The world is waiting to know what will come out of today's event. This is an extraordinary moment that requires extraordinary action. The world depends on us and on what we do. Whatever we do has to be exemplary, above and beyond. One of the exigent qualities for those sprinting for the possession of our national leadership is the acquisition of character and intelligence. You don't want a leader whose credibility constrains what you want this country to be. Our mission and vision must be demonstrated in style and value. I don't have an iota of doubt in my mind that all of you are identifying with what I am saying."

"Yes—we—are! Yes—we—are!" the crowd roared. "Yes—we—are!"

"I am here today because we are in a turbulent time. It is not the best moment to dream but to make quick decisions, and to talk about ourselves and our common problems. But we cannot talk about ourselves without talking about our country and ordinary citizens. We cannot talk about our country without talking about the people we voted into office who went there to represent themselves instead of the people. You and I have tried to be responsible citizens by voting in every election. They could not feel our pain and suffering, and are totally out of touch with us. You cannot see in your communities any significant evidence of anything from your representatives, which shows they have no true vision and goals for us. They don't like to be criticized, and they excel when nothing is achieved.

"The time has come to commit to a new rule of change, a moment to correct the structural imbalance that has dominated our system for so long. The challenge at hand—and it is urgent—is to identify the ignored, the circumvented, and the undignified. Our best reasons would be to revert and redirect our destiny, inspire confidence in ourselves and our children, and keep enthusiasm alive.

"What do we do?" Alex asked.

"Let them go. Throw them away," the crowd responded.

"I do not want to create the impression of being disrespectful to our political leaders or our political system. Our leaders at the capital are all honorable, and some of them are from noble origins," Alex said, flattering them. "It wouldn't be good to disturb their peace, or appear to be attention seekers, even when our complaints have been obviously indescribable and the source of unending agony. If you move from coast to coast, mountain to valley or anywhere in between, the results are the same. It doesn't mean that we expected miracles from them, though we never lacked the resources for that, but that they make deceitful promises during their loquacious campaigns. When they get into office, they worry about their lofty dreams, which they build on our backs, deepening our pain. Who would blame you if your confidence in them kept eroding fast?"

"Let them go. Let them go."

"Let them go. Let them go," the crowd roared again.

"They are not honorable," Ade said to his friends.

"They lied to us to get our votes," Uwa said.

"We elected them honorably and they got there to be dishonorable," Collin said.

"They cannot go to jail," Shola said.

"Because their friends are lawyers and judges," Ade said.

"Their government is full of tears and sorrows," Uwa said.

"Yes. Economic turmoil and political paralysis," Onu added.

"They are like the tax people," Eze said.

"No. Worse than the tax people," Amber said.

"You never see them in religious buildings," Brian said.

"Yes, they go during the election to seek support," Liz said.

"We need a revolution," Ade said.

"Let there be a revolution," Uwa affirmed.

"This is the only forceful means we have left to express ourselves. We have to come out en masse to show our thinking and will," Eze said.

"It's the only way out," Shola said.

"We cannot forget for a moment that these people have betrayed the trust of their constituents and the country," Brian said. "Let's get rid of them."

"Revolution, revolution!" Ade called out.

"Rebellion," Uwa said.

"Mutiny," Collin said.

"Revolt," Shola said.

"Let's walk and run to their places. Go to the House or Senate," Ade said.

"No. Everybody to the president's house," Terry said.

"We will demonstrate all day," Liz said.

"All week," Terry said.

"Until all of them leave the capital," Ade said.

"Let's go with our placards," Amber said.

"Yes, placards, placards!" Liz said.

"We will write 'Let the Politicians Go,'" Brian said.

"And 'No More Hunger,'" Ade added.

"And 'No More Taxes,'" Uwa said.

"We cannot …"

"Let's hear Alex speak," Onu cautioned.

"We cannot blame them for going there, becoming too comfortable and reluctant to know or understand what ordinary citizens are suffering in this country," Alex continued. "I should blame myself and you the citizens for being quiet for too long. We have exercised patience and perseverance for too long. We have been docile enough in the face of their attitudes.

"My fellow countrymen and countrywomen, if I should move your feelings and your emotions, I would tell you that we should stay at this capital until they listen to us."

"We'll stay! We'll stay! We'll stay!" the crowd roared.

"We must flow with this tide or we will lose it forever. You have taken pains to be here today, and you should take exceptional advantage of it. This is our last stop to have a symbol of honor and hope and an unpolluted democratic mind and humility. Today, you have an opportunity and a big responsibility to act with reason and judge with wisdom. True opportunities knock but once, as was said. The rest of the time, you create them."

While Alex was talking, the crowd was temporarily quiet, as if everyone had left the scene. The drop of a pin could have been heard. People were listening attentively and waiting to rush out for the demonstration. Reaction had been swift and fierce. Alex held them back while playing on the strings of their hearts, unfolding their frustration and tremendous concerns, and all the affairs of the country. Having captivated their minds and spirit, he catapulted them into the position of making an unshakable demand that would benefit the country. He induced them to ask for a strong character for the leadership, and a person of excellent knowledge, conviction, and aspirations as prerequisite qualifications to occupy the office of the president.

"Whenever you meet the leaders at the capital," Alex asserted, "be careful, because they will consider you a nuisance. You could be arrested and jailed. They have been worried about their security. Their behaviors never manifest any true love or patriotism for the country."

"Speak for us," Terry said.

"They are liars," Ade said.

"We will get every one of them," Uwa declared.

"They make slavish promises and policies," Collin said.

"Thinking we could never organize as a people," Liz said.

"Cheaters!" Shola shouted.

"Deceivers!" Liz added.

"Untrustworthy people," Ade said. "Corrupt and dirty."

"They operate with other people's money, thinking they have powers that are unreachable by ordinary citizens," Uwa said.

"Arrest them and put them in jail," Onu said.

"But they are lawmakers," Bill said.

"They made laws to favor their friends and families. They have shallow, self-serving interests, just satisfying the priorities of their immediate relations. Their kinsmen are above the law," Ade said.

"Heartbreakers," Shola said.

"They add to the burden of the people," Liz said.

"And they will ask you to bear with them, and want you to show more understanding and tolerance," Onu said.

"They don't like to be challenged or asked questions. Their answers are mostly vague or ambiguous," Liz said.

"Living large and making the taxpayers and the poor pay the bills. The powerless have been suffering in misery and anger," Onu said.

"Let no one vote for them again," Amber said.

"Let's bring them together and force them to resign en masse," Ade said.

"Let's go, my people," Onu requested.

"People have exhausted both their resources and their patience," Eze said. "This is a grassroots opposition and will be a lesson to all the elected or appointed officials at the capital and throughout the country. It is something they will remember even when we're gone. We trusted them with leadership, and they failed us. Most of the citizens feel hopeless, helpless, and unprepared to respond. We wanted to do something but didn't know how to do it. Our thanks go to Alex, who has used this period of election to address our problems. Good timing."

"I am a little curious. Who's this Alex? Do we know him from before? I can't remember hearing about him," Gboko asked the people around him.

"What good is that question?" Shola responded. "Well, the answer is that he is not a politician. He says things exactly way they are. We know what he is talking about, and we know he is saying the truth. I hope you're satisfied now."

"Before you step … " Alex continued.

"Wait, ladies and gentlemen. Alex is still talking," Shola said.

"Before you step forward, I want you to have a clear and defined direction of where you're going. There are people out there who would stop at nothing to dampen your zeal and fight to keep things the way they have always been. These people's interests are at stake. This country could have been better than it has been. One thing that is crystal clear is that this country is wonderfully blessed with immense wealth and resources. This is not a country where a piece of cake would be enough for everyone. We have momentous and unmatched opportunities that are being misused.

"Our pride, honor, and dignity are at stake. This country used to provide innumerable jobs and protections for her citizens and immigrants. Every country in the world wanted to be our friend. People all over the world respected and honored us with indulgence. Nothing seemed to be lacking. Why then do we fold our hands and watch this great country go downhill? If we should defeat the fear to act, we would defeat our political wreckage and impotency. Every cancer needs a radical treatment; time and tide wait for nobody. We have to arise to recover our rights and our stolen luxury."

"Let us march to the president, senators, and the House of Representatives," Ade requested.

"Wait, Alex is still talking," Liz said.

"Everything we hoped for—economy, welfare, education, agricultural development, sports, and entrepreneurship—has been derailed," Alex said. "All our colleges, schools, bridges, and other infrastructure could have been upgraded with modern technologies, just to name a few projects. Now we are heading nowhere. They lack transparency because they misappropriate our money. When it was proved that they lied to the people, they said they misspoke. They are like snakes with forked tongues. Various reasons have been given for the economic failure, and they blamed everybody except themselves. Your taxes are raised, but their own money and businesses are moved offshore. They live in mansions and drive exotic cars, make bogus allowances for frivolous trips. They didn't leave enough money to build roads and bridges for their constituencies. There are not enough books and there is not enough equipment at the libraries. We have been left at the pleasure of the political godfathers rewarded handsomely with resources meant for the citizens. It's a thing of great national concern when our future is in the hands of unprincipled individuals."

"No more! Never again!" the crowd shouted.

"This is a nation where our politicians always promise to be more transparent and productive, create a lot of jobs, and reduce taxes. But all these were mere sentimentality and erratic promises—mystic hope. They kissed babies on the street during the campaign and swore to defend the constitution; they looked citizens in the eye and lied to them, knowing full well that those promises would never be realized—sugarcoated words and encouragement to appease the voters. The government has become unjust when the leaders cannot demonstrate a simple sense of honor. It is astonishing and inconceivable that we could be looking forward, expecting something better under these awful, retarding, and stagnating circumstances."

There was loud applause, and then it was quiet again.

"Sometimes I feel like crying when I think about the systematic oppression, how the leaders to whom we gave our votes wandered and stayed away from their constituents and the country without thinking about the bondage of a bad economy, unemployment, the hunger and anger of the citizens," Alex continued. "They used their positions to control the citizens' means of survival and provided only for their friends, families, and cronies. The electoral machine has been turned into a franchise where the wealthy choose who they want in the government and for how long. With their high degrees of financial influence, the right candidates with less money have fallen like a pack of cards. It looks like we're practicing two systems of democracy: one based on wealth and influence, and the other based on the people when they are given the opportunity to exercise their voting rights.

"We place boundless trust and complete affairs into the hands of the men and women considered to be of eminence and distinction. The electorates and the entire citizenry applauded them when they won, thinking it was a real victory for all. No! Nothing encouraging or satisfactory came out of it. Solving this problem of great magnitude and multiplication should not be delayed any longer for you and me. The citizens should find a solution through the constitutional power they possess."

THE CROWD

"We are here because we want to be seen and heard from. We have been treated wrongly and unjustly. We demand our government back," Alex continued.

"Yeaaaaaaah!" the crowd roared.

"The government of the people, by the people, and for the people. We should have equal justice, opportunity, and equal class of citizenship."

"Yeaaaaaaah!"

"No more rewards to friends and relations, lobbying and appeasement for and to the political associates who have compromised the system we trusted dearly and endeavored to hold high. We cannot allow this dangerous drifting and their behavioral degradation to continue ad infinitum.

"The citizens must conquer this monumental and historical injustice that has started to overshadow our means and our future; this gridlock and monstrous politicking has to be laid to rest. They exist at the expense of the citizens, making them entertain fear and prejudice. There is no doubt that rebellion springs from discontent and desperation, followed by involuntary and irresistible impulses that call for a cause.

"Are you with me?" Alex asked.

"Yeeeeeeeeeessssss," the crowd responded.

"Do not dwell too long on national setbacks and failures. We have to push forward. In the face of all the challenges, you wouldn't choose to resign or give up, but to tackle the obstacles. Do we give up?" Alex asked.

"Noooooooooooooooo," the crowd said.

"Do we surrender?" Alex asked.

"Noooooooooooooooo," the crowd said.

"It means that we must move diligently to overcome this moment of turbulence and stampede. We have to do it together. You know the saying that two groups make up the theater: the performers and the audience. Each one needs the other.

"It's great to be with you here today. I can't express myself well enough, but I am piously grateful that you all made the sacrifice to be here. I will keep thanking you. The fundamental choice today is to invigorate our causes, and the causes are the liberties and freedom we have and should enjoy like no other place in this universe. We have to maintain these values at our own time so that our children and grandchildren will inherit them. Our sovereignty and independence are the most incomparable glory any generation can inherit. All these make other people of the world pledge allegiance to our flag. This inheritance left for us by our ancestors is the utmost mark of civilization."

There was loud applause and then the singing of the national anthem.

"I have a deep faith in the destiny of our nation," Alex continued. "We have the means and the ability to abolish poverty in this country and care for our veterans and children. It would not be a point of pride if a country were wealthy and her citizens could not live their lives to their fullest potential. There are people who make things happen and others who wait for things to happen. Life means different things to different individuals. One thing that may be common is that everyone wants to be happy. We have to draw inspiration from noble minds, our ancestors who acquired and then sustained the credibility and stability of this, our great nation. Their blood of martyrdom watered the tree of our liberty."

The crowd applauded.

"I am not speaking here today to excite hatred. That would be a poor way of effecting a reunion of hearts and to answer these exigencies of stimulated national consciousness. This is a message of the golden future and will be passed on to those who come after us. We are having a dynamic movement that promotes our sharing of the same fears and aspirations. The cardinal feature is to preserve the feelings that we are the history of this nation and should defend our noble tradition. Looking at the crystal ball into an unknown future sometimes requires that we entertain venomous malice and control our temperament. We have to know that a lack of discipline and irrational reaction are not assets to our cause. My humble opinion is that violent means are not necessary. Constitutional channels exist and would sit better in people's hearts. It wouldn't seem in the court of manners that justice should be wrestled by violent means. Whatever we have lost can be recuperated by skilled methods, courage and wisdom, strength and vigor, and we will continue to excel."

The applause was long and loud.

"We don't need a rocket scientist to tell us that we would soon get out of this fog if we could keep to our causes. Let me make it clear: the process by which to accomplish our means is confined to narrow bounds, but our determination has no limits. As a matter of serious importance, I would help extinguish the fire. Life without hope is full of inexpressible anguish. We have to invest in ourselves and the future of our children, and give unmatched dreams. People fear poverty; why shouldn't they? We should be concerned, mostly in this country where God has given us everything to live above the poverty level, unlocking potential and value."

There was loud applause.

"This country should be a place where all citizens can live out their dreams. It is certain that we have come to a time when our inner strength should raise us beyond and above, accomplishing our potential and meaningful things. Being part of this beautiful union has required unrelenting pain and endurance. Everything may not be for us, but in the quest for meaning, the benefit comes in the lives of our children and grandchildren, and with dignity and unselfishness.

"The time has come when men and women of great thought and action will arise. This is our country, and we are taking it back. The demand is not a dream but a reality. We will approach with caution. Let us not destroy in others what we are trying to build in ourselves. This country has the best democracy in the universe, and we are obliged to sustain it for ourselves, our children, and our grandchildren. All we are asking is to have a leader who cares about and listens to us, who bears with us in times of challenges and difficulties. We want someone who works from the heart without expecting political rewards."

The crowd applauded.

"The person cannot be overly ambitious or narrow minded, or do things for mere political value. He or she should be able to unlock people's opportunities and the potential for everyone to return to their former glories, and invest in the future of the young generation. This motivation has to be personal, natural, and positive. This is a gift God has given us freely, and without reservation. We should be thankful to God for this privilege, and have the drive to bring long-lasting hope and optimism to the citizens of this nation all the time.

"The election is just few months away. Let's nominate and vote for a rightful leader. Despite having such unprecedented concern at this uncertain time and in this tumultuous climate, it is your indisputable right to choose your leaders through your voting process. We will jointly support the growth of democracy. We have heard and know that you cannot use force to spread democracy, but you can use force to protect it. This country is unique, and wonderfully so. We can never be sorry for what we are and have been. You will all go home in peace and reflect on everything I have said. Be patient till the end. We have come this far and cannot destroy the system now. If you want me to be your president, I will be your voice."

"You are the president! You are the president! Alex is the president!" the crowd roared.

It turned into a song, and they rushed to his podium and lifted him high. People were singing and dancing, and they screamed at the top of their voices: "Long live the president! Long live the president! Long live Alex the president!"

When the songs slowed down and he was given the opportunity to continue his speech, he tried to conclude: "Thank you very much. I will be your voice if chosen. I will never allow your pains to go in vain. It will never happen again in this country that our leaders will be allowed to chase shadows, when a ringworm is treated even when leprosy is consuming the body. Looking into your hearts and minds, I know most of you are feeling sour, especially about our politicians, who are possessed with unusual pride and fail to do their jobs. In the process of nourishing their power and ego, they became numbed to the reasons and feelings of the ordinary citizens and the country. We have to embark on a new method of discarding the old ideas and strategies that have not been working. The only thing that should be a victory for me is be to see the citizens happy again, considering with uttermost seriousness the choices and decisions that will renew our greatness as it used to be. Most importantly, refocusing on strong, authentic values, and making sure this beautiful nation doesn't drift back to any disaster or state of fears."

The applause was loud.

"This beautiful nation will rise above the cloud of inequality. We will reconcile the most humble with the vitalizing citizens because it is right and necessary. It is being said that equality is only for those who are equals but, this country must be seen as a whole country of equality for all citizens, and not classes of equals."

He stopped while the people clapped.

"The days are gone when certain people put themselves in positions where they could not be challenged. You the people solely and exclusively have unchallengeable power."

There was loud, long applause.

"We cannot live in fear, with crime skyrocketing and citizens sleeping with their guns and their alarm systems turned on 24/7. These are some of our doubts and weaknesses that must be tackled with strength of will. We judged our leaders by their behaviors, and how we lived and how we should live. Even when it seems like we are living better than other nations, you and I should send the message, demonstrating to the people in government that we are the power, we are the nation builders. In the alternative, the gravest error of continuing with the paralyzing pattern will make the anger of the citizens rise high and higher until an outlet is provided.

"Here is a nation that is made great through individual contributions and sacrifices, and not by individual domination. Personal desires should be discarded, and the affairs of this nation should be better when taken away from the hands of the people whose passionate ambition has been their pleasure and luxury. In the forum of conscience and profound conviction, we should not continue to leave our affairs in the hands of people we cannot believe to be sincere. Our general interest should always be a priority. Any person who wants to lead this country should not be greedy or selfish. The person must love and work for this country with all his or her heart. All the politicians are well paid for their jobs, but they should not be arrogant themselves, living above everyone both in prestige and recognition. Anyone who cares for us and about us should demonstrate that he or she is of noble ideas and ideals. This is not a nation where good performance comes about by accident, but by hard work, willingness, and persistence."

There was more loud applause.

"My relentless pursuit and desired ultimate triumph is to restore our cultural identity and unadulterated patriotism. Our daily behavior and activities must be geared toward making ourselves and our nation the best of all times, stretching our goodwill to the remotest part of the world. That's a wonderful sentiment, and that's the indisputable way of having peace within us. Peace is the epitome of civilization. And civilization without peace has no virtue. It's been said, and we know too, that war has never been a symbol of civilization. Some think that making peace only in another country will bring peace at home, and to some degree, yes, that is true. Because of some politicians' erratic behaviors, we have the joke that the politician who is intelligent has no morals and the one who has morals is not intelligent. The fundamental goal is to have peace here before we can export it to other countries."

Alex was interrupted with loud applause.

"This is a unique country with a unique military, with sailors and air force personnel of intellect and fortitude, and with unquestionable integrity and valor. They can do any job delegated to them here and abroad, including peace making. Our pride and honor would be to have enough of this peace within us, showing some compassion and human decency and being charitable to our fellow citizens.

"Awake your senses, ladies and gentlemen, and use your glorious moments and unrestricted freedom to secure harmony and fraternal kindness for ourselves, our children, and our grandchildren. The development of our nation cannot be done by those with misguided zeal, who turned out to be masters instead of servants of the people. They abuse our patience. Our prominence and civilization have been pushed to the tipping point. The quickest and most determined way to restrain this progressive deterioration is to make active and positive efforts to preserve our core values. We feel alarmed and threatened by our own behaviors. No other nation in the universe would threaten us. We do not envy anybody other than ourselves."

The applause was loud and long.

"It will be a great error, pretending to be ignorant of the unresponsiveness and the unaccountable behavior of this present government. We are citizens with generous hearts and noble spirits, but there is no second thought that every citizen wanted a government with a noble aspiration and transparent behavior. You are the force that can unequivocally cause the instrument of change to revolve. If this reunion of government is not working, we need to reset it."

"Reset! Reset! Reset!"

"Reset! Reset! Reset!" the crowd roared.

"The time has come. This is the moment when the wheel of justice and the bearing of exigencies will no longer depend on whom you know. Obviously, some of you are enduring some bitterness and impatience when the regular comfort of life seems unreachable. Simple amenities are scarce, and when available, seem to be a privilege.

"You and I are sick and tired of people being put in positions because of their family money and influence, knowing full well that they don't have the competence or skills to sustain public confidence or approval. We have a surfeit of people with transparent stewardship and accountability who should be given opportunities to serve in our important offices. There is no force stronger than the people, and we should show that we are in control.

"Taking a common pledge to denounce a system bristling with obstacles sounds like a good idea. It is a responsibility we should take with ardor and devotion. None of us would die and rest in peace if we left this world without making this country better than we found it. The story of this country is found in the collective stories of our grandparents, you and me, and our children."

There was loud and long cheering.

"I have no doubt in my mind that you all know that the greatness of this nation didn't come by accident. No one here would disagree that our grandparents disposed themselves willingly through the long, hard times and difficult places to secure what we are enjoying freely. They knew that failure was not an option. Should we allow this hard-earned value to crash and burn?"

"No! No! No! No-o-o-o-o-o-o!"

"No! No! No! No-o-o-o-o-o-o!"

"No! No! No! No-o-o-o-o-o-o!"

"Should we protect our values?" Alex asked.

"Forever—forever and more!"

"Forever—forever and more!"

"Our success would be apparent and visible," Alex said.

"Yeaaaaaaaaaah!" the crowd responded.

The crowd continued to grow louder as Alex aroused their sentiments.

"Our victory would bring happiness to all," he said.

"Yeaaaaaaaaaah!"

"And fulfillment?" Alex asked.

"Yeaaaaaaaaaah!" the crowd called, following up with loud applause.

"We must be excited, because something new is going to happen soon," Alex said.

"Yeaaaaaaaaah!"

"Our president would be supercharged and dignified."

"Yeaaaaaaaaah!"

"Our presidency would never be grab and run," Alex said.

"Never! Never again!" There was loud applause.

"The Senate would never be grab and run."

"Never! Never again!"

"The House would never be grab and run."

"Never! Never again!"

"No political office would be grab and run."

"Never! Never again."

"No more poverty," Alex said.

"Never! Never ever!"

"No more unemployment."

"Never! Never ever!"

"No more inequality."

"Never! Never ever!"

"No more ruptured political system."

"Never! Never ever!"

"No more offshore laundering of stolen national treasures."

"Never! Never ever!" There was loud applause.

"No more elusive and unfulfilled promises."

"Never! Never ever!"

"No more deception."

"Never! Never ever!"

"Workers' rights and privileges must be respected."

"Ever and ever."

"Always number one in the world."

"Ever and ever."

"Have good jobs."

"Yeaaaaaaah!"

"The best education for our children."

"Yeaaaaaaah!" Applause broke out again.

"The best health care for us and our families."

"Yeaaaaaaah!" There was more applause.

"No more begging for the bare necessities of life."

"Yeaaaaaaah!"

"We are tired of party greed and strife."

"Yeaaaaaaah!" The applause was loud.

ALEX SUPPORTERS

"The fabric of our laws will not be twisted again by those we elected to safeguard them," Alex continued.

"Yeaaaaaaah!"

"These are our values!"

"Yeaaaaaaah!"

"Aspirations!"

"Yeaaaaaaah!"

"Nonnegotiable!"

"Ever and ever."

The applause and cheering were loud and long.

"Thank you very, very much. Go home—go in peace. Go back to your respective communities; choose and vote for your president and others. The problems of this great nation shall never be the same again," Alex concluded.

Loud applause was followed by the singing of the national anthem.

The crowd responded well, dispersing gradually and heading back to their respective homes. Capital National Park, which had seemed like an arena for the opening of the Olympic Games, was deserted in a few hours. Alex was given generous support, pomp, and ceremony. He had challenged his listeners to make tremendous sacrifices when they got home. He expected to get a reaction from the populace he had set on fire with his rhetoric. He had told them that this nation had never been surpassed in any way by any country. Despite being careful in what he said about the current government, he had exposed some franchising in the political system that engulfed the leadership and weakened the quality and decency of their services. He insinuated that the worst in their country was the best in other countries. Throughout the time, he had demonstrated unwavering strength and expediency, arousing his audience's minds and hearts to unimaginable and unparalleled emotional levels.

There had been constant applause and standing ovations. Some people had cried openly and requested a revolution. Alex had seemed to be supporting their desires when the tempo was high, but had gradually sprinkled some cold water that voluntarily or involuntarily brought the fire to ashes. It had been a glorious enterprise. His influence and the power of his speech had not been interrupted except by applause and cheering. He had used his weapon lavishly, which had captured the souls and minds of all the people present.

He was very charismatic and incredibly calm, with zeal and wisdom. He easily convinced everyone in the crowd to go home, and they agreed with one mind that the electoral process was the ideal democratic means by which to make a change. There was an incredible opportunity to start a revolution if he wanted to force himself into national leadership, but he had demonstrated some courage and fidelity, and the unblemished reputation of our liberty and democracy to reciprocate goodwill.

Defending sovereignty and liberty was the highest legacy he said the citizens had inherited from their grandfathers, which made them spread their wings wide and fly like an eagle.

9

THE PRESIDENT AND HIS CABINET

Three days later, the president convened his cabinet to review what had happened at the Capital National Park rally. All of them were unaware of what had really happened, including the National Security group. It was such an unprecedented event that it took them by surprise. There was a lot of panic, and everyone was asking what was going on. The president manifested his fear, explaining how he and his family were hiding somewhere at the presidential palace when the information came that the event at the capital could spill over to unknown areas. He was concerned about what the national security chief was doing, whether there was adequate control of the rally, and whether the security agents were working closely with the attorney general. He was also worried about the situation of other government officials. The chief officer was asked to explain what had happened.

"Thank you, Your Excellency, and all of you cabinet members. Please accept my apologies for what happened at Capital National Park. It was just a usual event that ended in an unusual manner. The security personnel were ready, able, and willing to do their regular jobs, including the keeping of a contingency backup for a bigger crowd. This is what we do on a regular basis when any group of citizens is coming to the capital. At this time, unfortunately, the unexpected happened, not only to us but to the entire nation.

"We investigated the chief speaker and his affiliates when we got their application to use National Park for that date. There was nothing suspicious about them. The man Alex was a community person, humble and well liked for his work with youths and young adults. There was no record of any political or social fanaticism about any of them. A clearance for the gathering was given, and security prepared for them. Mr. Alex, who was the exclusive speaker, talked strongly and persuasively for a long time. The crowd started reacting abnormally at some point. Though he used some sentimental expressions, his speech wasn't really inciting. It isn't unusual to have powerful public speakers during rallies of this kind. His speech was recorded. Emotions were high, but there was no violence."

"The attorney general needs to review the speech to check if Alex violated his privilege to use the permit for such a rally at National Park and to check if there was any incitement in Alex's speech," the first Cabinet member said. "There could be an arrest; we don't know for sure."

"Was it a political, social rally or what? Is he running for any position?" the second Cabinet member asked.

"Are we going to evoke emergency rules in this country now because of one man who came to National Park to express himself?" the third Cabinet member queried.

"I heard there was a point at which people were shouting for revolution and mutiny, and wanted to march to the president, the Senate, and the House," the second Cabinet member said. "Some wanted every elected member to resign or be sacked. What other incitement are we looking for?"

"We were called all kinds of names, including by people who don't have the future of this nation in their minds," the first Cabinet member said. "That's annoying. If they had not been restrained, that could have caused a lot of destruction and/or loss of lives."

"We have to be careful here, said the fourth Cabinet member. "Election is knocking at the doors, and any harsh action taken now could be misconstrued. Again, I heard the gentleman has built a formidable political force all over the nation since they left here. What he said at the rally has created a great commotion among us, but I don't think he broke any laws. The attorney general will soon explain it more fully. The fundamental and challenging task for this government now, with all courtesy, is to react reasonably to what is happening. We seem to have escaped from a lightning strike. It doesn't happen every time, but it's a reality. What happened should be the voice of the people, and it is coming forcefully. Are we going to listen to them or be in denial?"

PRESIDENTIAL MEETING

"The loss of freedom of assembly and the loss of courage to express ourselves openly, loudly, and freely would be the most disastrous thing that could happen to this nation," the fifth Cabinet member said. "I would not be part of it. Let's say we escaped the lightning strike as someone said. We should acknowledge the danger and demonstrate that we have blood in our nerves. The quick and eruptive reaction of the people from Alex's message indicates that the people have been in pain all these years, maybe because of governmental inadequacies. Unfortunately, the election will soon be here, and we need to go back to the same constituencies to seek their votes—that's hypocritical."

"Let us hear from the attorney general," the president said. "His opinion may clarify the technicality of what everyone is saying, and I would express my definite position. I wanted to make this meeting as brief as possible and explain to this cabinet what I intend to do."

"Thank you, His Excellency and honorable members," the attorney general said. "There's no doubt that this present moment has been tumultuous. It doesn't seem to be a good time for politics. In the early briefing I received, this government was portrayed as a political Sodom, regardless of whether it's true. Bitter expressions were used, and it was insinuated that the public had lost its faith in its leaders. The challenging situation is that the totality of their behaviors and actions did not violate the laws. Some violent opinions orchestrated an irresistible review from my department, for better consideration, but our wish and objective findings were that the spirit of democracy was beating high.

"If we cannot provide and grant freedom at all levels, we have lost the quality of government we're mandated to protect. We would look tyrannical and unaffectionate if we arrested a man who was here at Capital National Park to manifest his thoughts and opinion. There would be no democracy without this fundamental virtue. The desire for equality, concession, and tolerance does not equate to questioning a person simply because government officials were scared.

"I know, Mr. President," the attorney general continued, "and all the executive members were safe; hence the security was equal to the task. There could have been charges if the story had gone beyond what we are talking about now. From the table of power, the fullest flowering of crisis is the allowing of power to feed itself. Justice and decency require that you work to the best of your ability even when the people you are working for do not appreciate your labor," he concluded.

"This is a wonderful meeting," the president started. "It is good that you all know where our nation is heading. All of you who spoke raised some important issues. The attorney general clarified matters that have been important to this administration. We worked hard, and I appreciate the sacrifices of each and every one of you. The tenure of this administration is at its tail end, and we don't know what will happen when the people go to the polls.

"I thank the attorney general for not being overzealous regarding the rally at National Park. Chief of security, I appreciate that you and the attorney general performed jointly with wisdom and integrity. There was a time when I thought that national security was threatened—a lot of uproar, applause, and jeering. I quickly retired to the emergency area of my building and stayed close to the telephone. I am glad it wasn't worse than that.

"For the sake of posterity, and for the stability and tranquility of our beloved nation, we cannot resort to violent remedies. Our pride, honor, and dignity could have been at stake. It's true that you all not only worked hard, but went beyond the call of your duties most of the time. In an ordinary life, especially in politics, people easily forget the times of merriment, but times of sorrow are never forgotten.

"The man at the rally, Alex," the president continued, "did what he was privileged to do. There are certain principles a free man must possess, and exercising free speech is part of it. The number of people at the rally was a clear indication of how much he was supported. It doesn't matter whether they congregated for political, social, or economic reasons. Nothing can exceed the power of the people. The event was unparalleled to what used to happen at the park. In the long run, this administration, which is being used as a springboard, will be glorified.

"The important information for you all is that I do not intend to run for this coming election. It would cause me mental and physical agony if, in trying to be politically correct, I ended up distorting people's hopes and dreams.

"The paramount subject for every good citizen is to be a guardian of our liberty. I don't want to sound like I am campaigning, but I know we have done a good job. We reduced the gap between the haves and the have-nots, improved the health system, collected more taxes from the rich and corporate institutions, and improved the educational system, and our economy is more buoyant. All of you should be proud of your noble jobs.

"The obvious reality of public life is that you cannot please everyone. We will all go home after the election. Be proud of your accomplishments. Some of you could come back with the next administration, and I challenge each and every one of you to continue with your impeccable service to your constituents and the nation. Politics is very attractive, but you must have a big heart to be in the game, and be courageous enough to exit at the right time. My supreme prediction is that it won't take too long for history to challenge the present developments.

"There is the saying that when your heart tells you something and your head tells you something else, you should ask yourself if you have a better head or a better heart. In light and life, this consecrated, formidable, unblemished, and inalienable system will be protected, and shall last for eternity. The schedule for the election will soon be published, and if any of you are running, I wish you good luck," the president concluded.

10

ED AND FRIENDS

Ayo left the rally with unpleasant feelings. He was swallowed by the magnitude of his disappointment and rage. Every round of applause during Alex's speech had hit him like debris from a crumbling house. He knew Ed would encounter insurmountable obstacles if he were to proceed with this political exercise. He shook his head and said, "It is over."

While still lamenting to himself, he added, "I am glad I attended this rally, because I could not have imagined what I saw and heard. This is incredible. It has heightened my concern. It won't make sense for Ed to tear himself into fragments for nothing."

When Ed and his friends heard that Ayo had attended the rally, they were happy. They quickly organized to meet with him. He was their best source to find out exactly what had happened at the Capital National Park rally. His information would be their best asset for forging ahead. All of Ed's friends came to hear from Ayo.

"My dear friends," he started, "this game seems to be over. I am not being pessimistic, but realistic. From the bottom of my heart, it doesn't look good." He continued to narrate his experiences and how he had made the late decision to attend, knowing the importance of getting accurate information about what was happening there.

"This Alex was phenomenal at the rally. I was almost holding my breathe to hear him talk. It was a spectacular moment, and he exhibited unusual eloquence, which fascinated his audience. It was an enormous gathering, which I believe surprised both him and the organizers. Judging from people's reactions in that environment, I don't think anything will stop him from being the next president of this country. He manifested unsinkable self-confidence, and the crowd received him with enthusiasm. His remarks were genuinely pacifying, forcing listeners of different dispositions to focus their unwavering curiosity on what is lacking in the present government. He was never deficient in words or courage to sway and influence the fragile feelings of his listeners, awaking them to action and disposition to take back their country. He acted like he was on a special mission. His commanding and intimidating voice uncharacteristically moved people to tears. At a certain point, he told them how he had served our country with a lot of heroes who never came back. He used expressions that would melt your bones. When he was finished, I was physically weak and emotionally drained." Ayo paused.

"Popularity, as people say, is a matter of luck, and you have to be smart to take the fullest advantage of it; Alex grabbed this opportunity with passion, and any person who challenges him will be crushed," Ayo continued.

"How could you be convinced so easily, with one day's rally?" Pepe asked.

"The man was shaking the ground like an earthquake," Ayo replied.

"Is it that serious?" Bob asked, sitting up from the sofa.

"More than serious," Ayo continued. "I have never witnessed a rally like that. I wouldn't have believed this story if I hadn't gone there. He was interrupted several times by long, loud applause and standing ovations. Some people were crying while he was talking. I froze up to my bone. He stirred people's emotions to unimaginable heights, and set them on fire. There was a clamor for revolution, rebellion, and mutiny. Yes, it was a rousing speech."

"What? A revolution?" Pepe asked, surprised.

"Yes, almost an uprising," Ayo quickly responded. "I can't even explain it well enough. It was like a powder keg waiting to be ignited. I believe that if all the senators, House representatives, and the president had known what was happening at Capital National Park, they wouldn't have stayed behind because of the risk of endangering their lives. The crowd was almost exploding, and a lot of people, especially politicians, could have been hurt if he hadn't made a soft landing. He spoke calmly and eloquently. With fairness and honesty, he said things that were captivating.

"In attendance at this rally were people from all walks of life. Some of them, like me, were curious, and others were fans and loyalists. He performed elegantly, with spectacular vigor. He continued persistently to demonstrate the excellent master skills of a great speaker. He gave everyone something to take home—courage, determination, and the ability to mobilize forces for their different constituencies.

"It was amazing how he energized such a multitude and challenged them vigorously for their patriotic commitments. Prospective candidates were placed at the altar of fear, and the only nonnegotiable means they could prevail on would mean they had to exit voluntarily with honor and dignity. He reminded his listeners that some politicians would come to them with sugarcoated words and ornamented promises, and he classified those promises as fantasies. When he asked if such individuals would be their expected leaders, the crowd roared, 'Noooooooooooo!'"

"And he ..." Bon wanted to ask a question.

"He was the only person who controlled the crowd," Ayo continued, as if he didn't want to be interrupted. "People didn't want to leave when he was talking because they wanted to hear every word that came out of his mouth. In the ordinary course of events, this man could not be a beginner. He was so illustrious and persuasive. At times, he rose like a tide, coming down ferociously and splashing evenly on the people. He touched everything from welfare, education, and veterans to the fight by our ancestors to secure and sustain our freedom and liberty. The aspect that chilled me the most was when he said that our ancestors used their blood to water the tree of liberty and freedom we are enjoying today. Anyone who went there was at one point or the other driven beyond his or her emotional bounds, and needed some mental emancipation to return to him- or herself. I am not his fan, but I learned something new from him." Ayo was pouring out his feelings now.

Ed and all his friends surrendered in their seats, losing their physical and spiritual holds. Ed was melting quickly like an ice cream cone in a hot weather. He believed Ayo, knowing there was no exaggeration in his statement. He knew how much effort and support Ayo had contributed to this political campaign. Ed's courage and reasoning was zigzagging in his heart and mind until he suddenly took a deep breath.

Laughing like a gambler who had lost all his money at the casino, Ed asked, "Where do we go from here?"

ED CONSULTING WITH FRIENDS

Everybody was quiet to avoid saying anything hurtful. Trying to shatter the long silence, Bassy threw in a joke, but no one in the room reacted positively. He said, suddenly, "I believe it's not Ed's time. It is clear and deeply obvious that this train has come to a final station."

"That's the cardinal reason why I went to Capital National Park," Ayo said. "I didn't want other people to tell me about the rally. I wouldn't have agreed myself if someone outside our group had come here to tell us these stories. I notice your sorrow and disaffection," he said, as if consoling Ed, "but what we are hearing is real and authentic. We can plan alternatively; otherwise we will become victims of what is being said when people's goals can be disastrous and unreasonable because warning signs are not heeded."

"We must congratulate Ayo for attending the rally," Ed said. "He brought lifesaving information to stop the accident of crashing blindly on the wall." Laughing childishly as if he was trying to get something off his mind, he waved his hand around and said, "History has been rewritten because what is happening now is not close to what we hear and know about our country. We have to be careful that we're not victims of circumstance. Alex seems to have the inclination of a tiger." He stopped without explaining why.

Turning to Ed to advise him, Gboko said, "Do not lose your will and vision. Do not be afraid of tomorrow. It might be bigger or smaller than today, depending on how we all prepare for it. You have to be assured that it will never be the same. There is the saying that people who are tolerant and can endure the most terrible afflictions will definitely see light at the end of the tunnel. This one is not really catastrophic but a learning experience. It wouldn't be the best of ideas scrambling with scanty means; rather, take advantage of this consolidated spirit to eye the future. But if Ed insists on continuing, I am ready to contribute my full support." Others were nodding in agreement as he concluded.

"You spoke favorably," Sy said, turning to Gboko. "What we're doing here is not a high school band rehearsal, but a serious matter of chasing the mantle of the highest office of the land. The duty we owe you as friends is to give you our ultimate support. Like every other game, if you win, we rejoice with you; if not, you will take it like a sportsman. We may be energized now to embrace the challenges that may come, but if we mean to continue, we must enter this game to win. Do we have all the logistics, substance, and direction to bring victory? Let's not play on sentiments. The illusion will be jumping on the bandwagon and knowing that the chance to win is minimal. Though you are inspired to run, my honest opinion is that this is an extraordinarily difficult time in which to actualize this dream. We have lost the advantage and may not recuperate easily."

"You said it all," Tony added. "It is not over until it is completely over. Though Alex has created this massive impression and hijacked the whole system, let's keep our fingers crossed and watch to see what comes of it. At the beginning, Alex didn't appear like a serious politician others should worry about. When I heard about his intended rally at Capital National Park, it had no relevance for me. It was like child's play. Here we are today, and things have changed. Whatever he said that made people to believe so much in him was beyond my comprehension."

"It hurts—I must tell you the truth," Ed asserted. "This is the first time I was seriously determined and energized to explore this opportunity. I was really hopeful about making headway. It quickly came to an abrupt end. Sanity has been thrown away in this coming election. Irrespective of all odds, you are all my heroes and my comfort. I am very proud of you. I would recuperate and wait for another chance, though I don't want to go to sleep with a pessimistic spirit. My humble reaction should not be misconstrued as submissive. We don't know exactly what Alex did to get to where he is. Even if he encountered divine intervention, we would find out.

"Thanks, guys, for your solidarity," Ed continued. "All of you have committed immensely on short notice. I really appreciate the goodwill. You have made history and will continue to make history that will have a lasting record. If you all could see a picture of my feeling, you would understand that my innermost expression frowns as if it would be an act of cowardice to surrender because of the fear of failing. A man should not be afraid to fall at any moment in time, but should be ready to rise each time he falls. I like taking positive actions in everything I do. After thinking deeply about getting involved in this race, I established for myself the valor and zeal to pursue it to a reasonable conclusion. However, this is not a one-man show. Let's look forward and not worry about the past; I will keep you all informed of any developments."

11

ED AND CONFIDANT

Ed went home thinking about what he had heard about Alex. He wondered how a single rally at Capital National Park could make every prospective candidate tremble like a leaf, and lose direction and aspiration. It was hard to swallow, but he wanted time to gradually reflect on it all. He began to accept the saying that there are certain times when life's circumstances overflow beyond one's control, sprinkling it with a lot of challenges. One could easily see one's self frustrated, feeling abandoned and heartbroken.

"That's okay," he said in his mind. "Life could easily get foggy or cloudy, mostly when it's least expected."

Soon after Ed got home and thought deeply about everything that had happened, including the opinion of his friends, he invited one of them whom he considered a confidant for a one-on-one discussion. His confidant came the following day as scheduled, and both of them sat to think more deeply about the situation at hand. Ed was sincere to him and expressed that he didn't want to give up the fight.

"You remember the Shakespearean saying that cowards die many times but the villain tastes death but once?" Ed asked.

His confidant nodded.

"That's how I feel now," Ed continued. "I have invited you so we could brainstorm on this important issue because I am emotionally fragmented and very vulnerable, based on the way things have developed. I want to resist any forces that would encourage me to surrender. Can you give me your perception in a nutshell and possibly how to navigate through this unfamiliar terrain?"

"I don't think you want to engage in this election because of any romantic or sentimental desires," his confidant said. "You have some values and ideals to accomplish. Stopping halfway would be the worst nightmare of your life, at least till the next election. There's no doubt that you're vulnerable now, and in politics, things can change at any moment. When the going gets tough, the tough get going. You've heard it before, right?"

"Sure!" Ed replied.

"Most importantly, you will be proud of trying even when the result is uncertain. It is a common saying that anything worth gaining must be gained with effort. This is a new frontier for you, but I know you are a hard nut. Ayo's attendance at the rally at Capital National Park was paramount to getting the information he brought to us, but if you are determined to move forward, you have to shield yourself with reason rather than emotion. I didn't want our last meeting to look argumentative, and irrespective of that, your position seemed to be resonating."

PRIVATE CONVERSATION

"Thank you so much," Ed interrupted. "It is on this premise that I invited you exclusively to get your considered opinion. This whole thing has been a roving conflict, almost like a roller coaster. You have always given me the noblest and most reassuring guidance during my difficult times. I am flabbergasted that an individual of untested skill could unwind the citizens' emotions, constructing in their thoughts an expression and impression that no other person could reasonably rule this country. It is phenomenal that all of us would succumb to his incendiary tongue. I will continue to give this discussion serious reflection, and you will be the first to know my decision. And I like your citation that anything worth gaining must be gained with effort."

After their discussion, both of them went to a nearby bar to have some beer before going to their respective homes. Ed was happy for his friend's profound contribution.

The issue of autism spectrum disorder had never gone out of Ed's mind, most especially because he had been asked about it at the town hall meeting. He had been wearing it like a medal, not because of his political values but to give a helping hand. Ed would help in fund raising for any organization taking care of these suffering children. Though the problem had been there for a long time, a lot of people like Ed still didn't have enough information about it. It was a matter of very important awareness derived from political encounters. He promised himself to show interest, do research on it, and get involved as much as he could in supporting all the groups involved in many ways to help these children. It had immeasurable humanitarian value.

A few weeks later, Ed was at a coffee shop during his lunch break and saw a young woman with a lot of health literature and a book about autism. He did not hesitate to ask her if she was a professor teaching a course on the subject. The woman politely told him she was in town to attend a conference on autism spectrum disorder. Ed demonstrated much interest in knowing more about this disorder. She was surprised that someone was suddenly asking about autism. However, she was delighted to talk about it. She took the opportunity to ask Ed if he had a child who was autistic. He replied that he didn't but explained that he was beginning to hear more about it. He didn't explain how he had been challenged on the issue at a town hall meeting. He had been thinking of ways and means by which to support the interests and activities relating to programs that helped children with autism. Ed expressed how he would volunteer his time as early as possible in drumming up support for these children. He later confessed to her how embarrassed he was the first time he was asked about it, saying he hadn't known what the questioners were talking about.

The woman, whom he learned was Ms. Bons, tried to explain how devastating the problem was and asserted that it was a neurodevelopmental illness, in a short term, complex type of disorder of brain development that was affecting millions of children in their country and all over the world. "It is more severe in some children than others; it has to be considered on a case-by-case basis," she explained. Lecturing further, she explained that some of the symptoms included verbal and nonverbal communication challenges. "Even with that, some kids have more difficult conditions than others. Some other common symptoms are emotional and aggressive behavior, with or without provocation; standing up and running away without any notice; moving around as if restless; problems staying seated for a prolonged time; difficulty playing with peers; a lack of a normal degree of affection or empathy—not understanding that they can hurt anybody; and an inability to exercise self-control or participate in constructive activities.

Some hate loud noises, and most of them have intellectual challenges. There are many other symptoms.

"One out of eighty children in the world is suffering from this disorder," she continued. "And the number is growing faster than we can imagine. Most of their parents are not prepared for these difficult challenges. Since autism has no cure, family members have no option besides adjusting their lives to deal with the problem. It's a long-term commitment. I could stay here the whole day talking about it."

"What are the causes of this disorder?" Ed inquired.

"No one knows. There have been a lot of theories and hypotheses, but no research has given a definite answer."

"I am shocked," Ed said. "I didn't know much about it until someone challenged me at a rally. Since then, my eyes and heart have opened to know more. It is baffling that it is affecting the lives of so many children and yet there is no cure. The awareness is minimal. Sometimes our priorities are misplaced. If the media could keep this information alive by talking about it regularly, like they talk about crimes and violence, obviously more people would know about it, and possibly, people with autism could receive more support. People are dying in silence."

"Yes, you are right," she answered.

"How long did your conference last?" he asked.

"It was a two-day conference and ended today," she replied.

"Oh, I would have loved to attend," Ed said. "I have an infinite desire now to participate in such conferences to educate myself more."

"That's okay. There are many of them at different places, although this one would have been more convenient for you because you reside in this city. If you don't mind, I will take your contact information so that I can notify you of other conferences coming up. I can also give you information about chapters of the Autism Spectrum Disorder Awareness Association around you and how to reach them. Some local communities and agencies were designed to promote awareness and develop strategies to help needy families get some support. It is a marathon race to find the best way to help these children, knowing there is no cure. Medication helps in certain ways, but the greatest challenge is coming up with reasonable behavioral modifications and therapies that will improve the lifestyles of these children."

Ed was surprised by how much he had learned from Ms. Bons in such a short time. He even forgot that his lunchtime was over. He walked back to his office thinking about the immense problems children were going through in his country while the majority of people did not know it.

The more he asked about it, the more difficult the answer became. No person prepares well for any illness, especially in children. The aspect that was not explained enough to him was the debilitating effects on the children's parents. He strongly suspected such parents were suffering enormously and encountering various severe social and economic challenges.

In fact, it was hard to measure the tremendous effect on parents, guardians, and loved ones. Despite living with a regular high level of stress and the severity of the pain of taking care of these children, the hope of finding solutions to their problems was not available. No one needed to be told how devastated and shattered any parent would feel, mostly watching little innocent children suffering from intellectual disabilities and struggling with speech, impulsivity, and aggressive behaviors. Again, having a lifelong condition seemed like long-term torture from nature. What was obvious to Ed now was that one's condition could easily be transformed by the vicissitudes of life. While juggling all these things in his mind, Ed could not resolve whether he would be better staying off in politics and committing himself to the efforts of getting relief for these children and their families.

12

ED VISITS A SCHOOL FOR CHILDREN WITH AUTISM

When Ed found out there was a school for children with autism about twenty miles from his office, he was excited and called to make an appointment for a visit. The director was happy that Ed was coming to see them. Both sides saw it as a good opportunity to meet. The school director saw his coming as an opportunity for exposure that would attract future support. Ed welcomed it as a new avenue by which to know more about autism. He thought about going with his wife, but Titi was not available on the date the school was scheduled to receive him.

On that day, he first went to the school office, where Ms. Craig, the office administrator, and Mr. Cole, the director, were waiting for him. They were happy to see him. What Ed didn't know was that they knew about his ambition to run in the next presidential election. It wasn't immediately made known to him. He introduced himself without mentioning politics. The only thing he asked was to visit some classrooms and spend some time with the teachers and students. The director wasn't comfortable with that, explaining how risky it would be to him. He explained to Ed that some of the children could physically attack him or throw objects at him without any provocation. Ed replied that he wasn't afraid of any injuries. He insisted that his visiting was to see things for himself because of what he had been hearing about autism. He confessed that he hadn't known much about it until someone confronted him with the issue at an event. The director granted his request but still cautioned him to be careful.

He was led to the first classroom, where he was introduced to the teacher. The director spoke briefly with the teacher before going back to his office. She offered Ed a seat near her table. He thanked her but told her he wanted to be close to the kids. It was a small classroom of about eight children between the ages of nine and fifteen. They had various challenges. Some were verbal, and others were partially verbal or nonverbal. The teacher talked to two of them but used sign language for the others. One or two of them were looking at her, and others seemed to be distracted by other things. There were three other teacher's assistants in the classroom, which was not enough for the number of children. But the staffing strength was the best the institution could afford. The director checked on Ed from time to time, though he had been told not to worry.

"Good morning, kids," the teacher started.

None of them responded.

"Can we say good morning to our visitor?" she asked.

One said, "Good morning." Another one waved after several prompts.

"Good job," the teacher praised them.

"Good morning, beautiful kids," Ed said. "Are you all happy to be in school today?"

Most of them were not focused, and the teacher's assistants struggled to redirect them to listen to the teacher and Ed.

One nodded yes while another said "No." The teacher, her assistants, and Ed laughed.

"I know you like school, don't you?" the teacher asked. The boy who had no before said yes.

"And today is pizza day, right? And with fries, which you like so much."

"Yes," the boy responded.

"Do you have any questions for our visitor, Mr. Ed?"

"What is your name?" the boy asked slowly.

"You are a very smart boy," Ed said as he gave the boy a high five. "My name is

Edward, but people call me Ed. And what's your own name?"

"I can't tell you because my mother told me not to talk to strangers." Everybody laughed.

"Your mom is right. Don't talk to strangers on the street. I am here in front of your teacher, though, so you can talk to me. If you don't want to tell me, that's fine too. I can call you the Handsome Boy."

"Nooo," he said, stamping his feet. "My name is not Handsome Boy."

"Fine," the teacher said. "Don't get upset about it. You can tell him your name another time. Do you have another question for him?"

The boy walked back to his chair without saying anything. The teacher was trying to explain that the boy, John, was one of the high-functioning kids in her classroom, but before she could conclude, another student got up from his chair and hit his peer, who was coloring some pictures. There was confusion, followed by the screaming and crying of the other child. Another child pushed down his desk and chair, and knocked down other things on the bookshelves around him.

One of the students called BJ suddenly ran out of the classroom, and one of the assistants followed him, leaving the teacher momentarily with only two other assistants. There wasn't any danger of the child running out of the building because the doors were safely locked, but they didn't want him to hurt himself or another child in the hallway, or allow him to run into another classroom. The boy could bite, scratch, or spit on any person when angry. The assistant stopped him in the hallway and brought him back to the classroom.

While the teacher was busy redirecting other children in the classroom who were not on task, one of them who was still throwing a tantrum threw his shoe at Ed's head, banging on the desk and screaming loudly.

"I am sorry," the teacher quickly apologized.

"That's okay. I am not worried about it. The kid is more important, as long as he doesn't hurt himself."

"That's not a good job, Charlie," the teacher said to the student. "You have the right to be angry but not to hurt people. Can you say sorry to Mr. Ed?"

"No," the boy said, banging his hands on his desk.

"Look, Handsome, you are hurting yourself," the teacher said. "If you break your hand, you won't have a hand to eat your pizza today. You know we are having pizza soon. Other kids will eat the whole pizza, and you can't eat with a broken hand. And your mum will be mad that you hurt yourself. Be a good boy now!"

Charlie immediately stopped banging on the desk and tried to stay calm.

"Can you pick up your shoe and say sorry to Mr. Ed?" the teacher asked. "If you lose your shoe in school, you will go home with one shoe; it won't look good."

Charlie picked up his shoe and hugged Ed. They clapped for him and the teacher, and Ed called him a good boy. Before the teacher could control all the issues in her classroom, she had scratches on her hands and the classroom was trashed with things thrown by the students. All her assistants helped to clean the room.

Soon after that, it was time for lunch. The problem started all over again. Some of the children sat nicely and ate their lunch, and two could eat only while sitting on the floor. One of them dipped his hands into his food and rubbed it on his body. One of the assistants intervened in time to save part of the food, and redirected the child to eat his food and not rub it on his body. Another child poured a bottle of water on the floor. At some point, the teacher seemed overwhelmed. All the adults started cleaning up again.

But there was one boy in the classroom who was just on his own, sitting away from the other children as if he wanted to be left alone. He was practically doing nothing, possibly waiting for the attention of the teacher or the assistants. This boy could not allow his peers to come to his desk. One unique thing he was doing was laughing alone, though nothing funny was happening in the classroom. When he stopped laughing, he began to cry. There was no provocation for the crying. He switched quickly from one feeling to another without any notice or known cause.

Some of the children seemed to be in diapers even at the ages of ten and above. Looking behind one of the students, Ed noticed that his diaper was soaked and hanging like a bag of ice. It wasn't as though the teacher or the assistants were ignoring him, but they had their hands full. The children had different severe problems in the same classroom.

Looking at such beautiful children with such difficult problems, one wondered why nature had been so cruel to these innocent ones, putting them in such a pathetic situation. The worst of all was that there was no cure for the disorder.

Ed was mesmerized by his experience at the school. He held his head in his hands, trying to assimilate the emotion that was descending on him like the dew. Everything he saw was more than he had expected.

"Do this kids behave like this every day?" Ed asked the teacher, curious.

"Some days are better than others," she replied.

Ed nodded, saying, "It's like you go home every day with scratches, blood, and sorrow."

"On difficult days, we may go home with scratches and blood, but not with sorrow," she said. "As humans, we feel the pain, but we try our best to show them love. No one can do this job without love for these children. You can see that we are understaffed—three assistants for eight children who need personalized assistants. We work as hard as we can to help these children. Some of them do not get enough support at home, and some parents may not be financially or emotionally stable enough to handle this challenging crisis. For those students, their best moments of the day are here in school. We try to make their lives as comfortable as possible within our means.

"Despite all the injuries I and my assistants sustain here, we don't hold the kids responsible. They do not know what they are doing. Some of them have mood swings: happy in this moment and physically and emotional aggressive a few minutes later. It is difficult to know the causes of all their problems. Some are medical, and others are irritated by sound, light, or movement. Some eat too much, and others eat too little. The most challenging ones are the nonverbal.

"It is hard to know when they are hungry or in pain. Though we teach them sign language and some functional skills, only a few of them benefit from them; others progress slowly. I do everything within my resources, including spending my paycheck to buy some of the things we use in this classroom. This program is not adequately funded, and we don't know who to blame anymore," she continued to explain.

"Some of these children function better than others. But we can only work with the little we have. It's good that you came here to see things for yourself. If others, especially public officials, could visit these children as you have done, it could make a big difference, and there might be a turnaround in the ways these children are supported. Look at these children and how beautiful they are. In fact, illness has no respect for beauty. I really hope that one day their plight will touch some people's hearts and they will realize that these children are suffering. We are a wealthy country, for goodness' sake," the teacher concluded.

Ed thanked the teacher for her hard work and kindness. He praised her for her loving service and care, and said he thought she was going beyond the call of duty. They shook hands, and Ed returned to the office of the director.

"Thanks again for spending your precious times with us today," the director said. "Now you have firsthand knowledge of what some of our children are going through in this country. We need a huge amount of support here. Some of these kids need equipment we cannot afford with our little resources. Politicians and other people who should help us have always given a million reasons why the money isn't available. We have invited some of them down here, but they never have time. The mayor would blame the governor, and the governor blames the president. At the end of the day, nothing is done and the children keep suffering. We love it when people like you come to visit us. If you win this election—and we wish you well—no one will tell you what this institution stands for."

"I appreciate the opportunity to visit this beautiful team of caregivers," Ed said. "I don't have the words to express the services your institution is rendering here. The problem you have is enormous, and your teachers and other staff are angels. The conditions of these children are incredibly challenging; I was moved to tears. In fact, this should be a national responsibility that requires urgent attention. My visit today is not because of the election. I am beginning to learn about autism, and I thought it necessary to spend a little time here with the children. You should be assured that this visit will not be in vain."

"It is our pleasure having you today," the director said. "We hope you will come again. A lot of other parents are struggling to register their kids here, but as you can see, we can accept only a limited number of children. The children's problems are growing, whereas the specialized institutions that should take care of them are few. The few institutions available lack meaningful resources. Unless something is done fast, the children will be left in a precarious condition by their government."

"It should not happen," Ed interrupted, "and no sane person would do it. And, no one would believe the conditions of these children unless they came here or went to any other school of this nature. No description is enough to convey the whole story. Their conditions are unbelievably severe. I feel for them and their parents."

Ed thanked the director and all his staff again. He also asked the director if he could write about the school in the local newspaper, since he was a contributing staff writer. The director replied that autism required urgent public attention and involvement in finding a solution to it, adding that writing about it could be part of the solution.

As Ed was about to leave, there was a loud noise of someone screaming, running, slamming doors, and banging on windows. A boy about twelve years old ran out from one of the classrooms. He quickly removed his clothes in the hallway and was naked. He was yelling at his teacher and others who were trying to stop him. Ed stood quietly as the teacher used every nice expression to persuade the boy to put on his clothes. He refused but changed his mind after a few more redirections. Before the student picked up his clothes, he peed on the floor. Ed shook his head and wished them good luck before departing.

On his way home, Ed murmured to himself that the problem of those children he had met in the school was both natural and a national crisis. He called one of his friends and narrated his experiences at the school for children with autism. "A lot of people are suffering and dying in silence. I am a father, and I know it would have been anguishing to find myself in such a situation. The government should declare this illness an epidemic and provide enough support. From the deepest place in my heart, I can declare that our government has dishonored the services to children with autism by not addressing their needs with our best efforts. Regardless of resources, the government of any country that does not educate her children adequately and provide responsibly for their health care should not claim any greatness," Ed concluded. He also suggested to his friends that they should be ready again for fund raising after the election for the exclusive support of helping children with autism.

13

THE CAMPAIGN

As the days passed and the election drew closer, there was no sign of anyone challenging Alex in the presidential contest. It was quickly established that he was registered as an independent to be the president. The political parties shied away from nominating a candidate. It was an unprecedented occurrence in the history of the nation when only a single candidate, technically, would be voted for. The news of the rally at Capital National Park swept like a tornado across the nation, dampening the zeal and morale of any other prospective candidates. People who had previously declared their interests in running withdrew, and those who had not been open about it muted their desires. The feeling was like the old story of a person standing on the tracks to stop a moving train. Surely, it would be disastrous. Potential candidates kept away, making Alex a more viable candidate.

Alex's name was everywhere, and people worked tirelessly to guarantee his victory. He had courage that didn't fail him and his exceeding eagerness boasted of a man of ample and honorable kindness. His fame and popularity secured him the sole nomination (at the moment) for the highest political office of the land, the presidency.

Ed had difficulty admitting that he would not win the election against the famous Alex. One of the things that bothered him most was that Alex had never been tested, and had never given any interviews or participated in any debates. Ed tried desperately to find a breakthrough to restart and move his campaign forward. He saw this opportunity when he collected all the information about autism; it drove him above his fears and concerns, injecting his confidence with the assurance that his agenda was a formidable one that would make a lot of changes and possibly lead him to victory.

He summoned his friends again for them to give his new idea a second thought. The issue of autism that had dampened his prior attempt would uplift it now to the top with more energy. He wanted to show a sense of purpose by demonstrating that he would replace people's fear with hope and make children's affairs his number one priority if elected. It was an issue no one could resist supporting. Things that affect our children and grandchildren expose us to the risks from which we will never recover. Their joys and sorrows should be a motivational engine that drives our common struggle and endeavor.

When his friends listened to his story about the children with autism, it sounded like a missed opportunity. A few of them refused to politicize autism spectrum disorder even as they agreed it was a concern that deserved high national awareness. Clem didn't think it was funny. He thought it wasn't the best time for it, not condemning the agenda but reacting to the backlash toward Ed, since he had never been an obvious activist or fundraiser for such an important program. His idea was that Ed should wait until he could be proud to show how he had positively affected the lives of those children and supported the organizations and agencies caring for them.

Despite all the frustration and setbacks, Ed was determined to register as a presidential candidate. He was ready to take the bull by the horns and face the consequences. He didn't want to be discouraged doing it or regret not accomplishing his heart's desires. He registered before the date and stayed officially on the ballot. Now it was between him and Alex. He knew his risks and his chances of winning. His friends had been frank with him, though his die-hard friends promised to stay with him even in a worst-case scenario.

It was a complicated moment for his other friends who were given this basket of raw eggs to hold. The uncertainty about how to start and how to persuade people to vote against the popular Alex was a rocky situation. It created mental agony and jeopardized the efforts of his loyalists to campaign. Despite all the odds, some of his friends and associates didn't give up on him, even when they knew they were not making sufficient headway. They frantically wrestled to get their messages out across the country while remaining optimistic that something good would come out of it.

Another problem for Ed was that his agenda was being handled erratically; the first thing was done last and the last thing done first—upside down. He could have joined the Autism Awareness group, establishing himself as supporting from the heart and not taking advantage of the system to advance his political career. Ordinarily, it might have been a good thing to talk about or to publicize the problem of autism spectrum disorder at public places to create more awareness. The children could have benefited from it. The rush now to make it part of a political campaign did not sound good, even if he was trying to attract sympathy and support.

Any person involved in this issue had to be genuine to get effective support. Anything about children got quick attention if properly implemented. It could have been a springboard for the campaign of someone who wanted to pursue the children's interest. Ed had not shown that he would be a president who would promote the children's agenda. It seemed too late to restart his campaign and to raise funds. Now it seemed like jumping out of an airplane without a parachute.

Ed's political amateurism constituted a weakness and failure both in planning and execution. He was left alone to make hard choices, at times with few friends. And his choices seemed disconnected to the fundamentals of the campaign, which left his close associates decimated. When you are on the wrong route, you can never get to your destination, no matter how far you travel or how much time you spend, unless you exit to correct yourself.

Ed's name was on the ballot because he had registered before the dateline. He was completely unpopular, but he and his friends hit the ground running. They relied on the solidarity of a few friends to make headway. He and his team stretched their campaign as much as they could. They traveled as far as they could, projecting Ed as the sovereign and the most adequate person with a noble spirit to meet the needs of the country. They talked to any person who wanted to listen, but few took them seriously. Most of them had made up their minds about whom to vote for. The media were slow to get involved in the election. It was amazing how detached they were, as if nothing was happening. Before they could be ready, the election would be over.

When it seemed like all hope for Ed was gone, one of his friends threw in a radical idea. He suggested that Ed take every minute left to campaign on university and college campuses. He was told to promise free education to all the students. It would be a quick way to get the elusive students' votes. It was presumed that most of them had not attended the rally at Capital National Park and didn't know much about Alex. Ed was told to concentrate his campaign on talking about education on the campuses as if it were the only thing he would do as president. He was strictly advised against having any town hall meetings. It had created a problem once and would be a big risk, considering the other problems he had. The emancipation of Alex had originated from a town hall meeting that went wrong, and nobody would forget it very easily.

There would be no debates; therefore, no one was going to ask how the free education would be implemented or paid for. All these ideas seemed magical to Ed. He expected all these last-minute efforts to guarantee his victory or bring him to its corridor. None of his supporters and associates could rid him of this idea, and they went into work immediately. Several arrangements were made through some student leaders at different campuses. Many of them didn't really know Alex, and others were undecided about their vote. Some students said their candidates had withdrawn and they were ready to choose between Alex and Ed. Interestingly, Alex was not campaigning, although his community soldiers were doing overtime. It was an unprecedented method of getting votes, just like the selection of the candidates had been.

Another history-making phenomenon in this election was the nonexistence of a running mate. Neither Alex nor Ed appointed one. They could do it after the election, but it was very unusual. However, none of the candidates was under pressure to pick one. The circumstances of the campaign didn't warrant people asking for a running mate since all the candidates were running exclusively on their own records.

Ed went ahead with the free education pledge, and it was good bait for the students, many of whom could not resist it. Those interested in free education wondered why the issue had not been a priority throughout the campaign. At the beginning, the election had seemed like a one-man show, until Ed started to surface. Many students had believed in the past that the government had not cared enough to support their education. Now that the issue of free education had come up, those students wanted to know which of the candidates would be more enthusiastic about it. Because Alex was not campaigning, it was difficult to get his reaction toward it. However, many students were curious to know his position.

At the campus rallies, Ed drew in his breath and fired up the students by telling them what they wanted to hear. He knew Alex wasn't going to have another rally and was not campaigning hard, though his militant supporters were all over the country. Since some of the students had not attended Alex's rally at National Park, Ed twisted their mind-set by using the weapon that meant the most to them: giving them free education. He told them that education wouldn't have been expensive if the government had done its homework right. Going further, he promised that education and children's services would be his priorities. He seemed to be making a colossal breakthrough with his strategy. It was a last-minute marathon, less than three weeks before the election, and his promises seemed to be resonating among the students.

The late successful move aroused a new energy in his camp. They were traveling to as many campuses as they could. The results seemed to be the same. His associates told him to stick to what he was saying, whether he intended to honor the promises or not. They knew something like an optical illusion was happening. All the real and artificial barriers he had been encountering from the beginning were vanishing gradually, at least momentarily. Some of the students listened to Ed as he talked about free education and the elimination of government waste, including the fighting of unnecessary wars, when the money could have been used to fund education at all levels. He promised vehemently that he knew everything it would take to bring fundamental changes in the universities and colleges. The students believed him passionately and surrendered to him involuntarily.

As the election drew closer, Ed started worrying again, for a different reason: mostly that the student numbers would not be enough to win. He wished he had more time to campaign, and more resources to move as fast as he wanted. This unexpected experience was tormenting him and would continue till election day. It's common knowledge among political practitioners that in the wilderness of politics, there are a lot of unknowns, including but not limited to knowing whether everything needed will be there till the end.

The campaign was taking a heavy financial toll on Ed, and his wife was getting worried about it. Nobody could do anything about it other than to keep borrowing until the campaign was over. It was like a ship in the middle of an ocean: it had to keep going because its survival depended on reaching the other shore, where it could anchor. From the inception of the campaign, Ed wanted to avoid any panic attack.

The consoling aspect of it was that he was seeing significant progress on his campaign and the puzzle seemed to be coming together. Still, it didn't keep him from worrying, including worrying about his physical exhaustion. The campaign was put in overdrive because of the new strategy of going to the campuses, which had been a late decision. He had also pushed his friends to their extreme limits and didn't want to push them any further.

With almost one week to go, Ed came back from one of his trips tired, and had difficulty sleeping. It seemed like there was nothing else to do to cover more ground. The progress they were making had not been enough to override Alex's diverse appeal to the populace so far. Ed sat down for a few minutes on the sofa and then got up again to open the windows of his living room. It was late at night to keep the window open, but he wanted the cool wind that was blowing gently at that quiet hour to bring him some solace. The moon was full, though the streetlights didn't allow him to appreciate the soft reflection. He got a glass of wine with a few cubes of ice and sat close to the window, wishing the daybreak would be delayed for several more hours. He needed more magical advice, as his head was swelling or seemed to be.

His wife, who was also struggling to sleep because of the anxiety of the election, came down to ask why her husband didn't want to go to bed. She first asked him if he was all right, and Ed responded that he was. She asked again if he had eaten, and he said he was fine. There was no doubt that it was a challenging time for both of them, but she realized from his tone and response that he preferred to be left alone. She went back to bed, telling herself that she should have listened to her intuition when she'd seen all these problems coming their way.

Ed sat back on the sofa, took his glass, and sipped a little wine. While he still had the glass in his hand, gazing into the unknown world, his mind wandered all over. He took a deep breath and sighed, and there was a smile on his face. Looking through the window again to the sky, he saw a multitude of stars. Though they seemed to be close to the earth, they were twinkling from millions of miles above. There was chirping sound from an owl and some other birds twittering from the woods behind his house, as if they were delivering a message. Fireflies hovered all over the front lawn, flashing their orange and purple colors. Without any doubt, it was the best time to cultivate the mind and to appreciate God's handiwork.

Suddenly, his phone rang, which was unusual for that late hour of the night. He startled, looked at it, and saw that the call was from one of his best friends. He wondered why he was calling at that odd hour of the night, knowing that they planned to meet the next morning. Reluctantly, he picked up the call. His friend said that someone had informed him that Alex was very sick. There wasn't enough information about what had happened to him, but the friend promised to investigate further before their scheduled meeting that next morning.

The call exacerbated Ed's anxiety. He didn't wish Alex ill but imagined what it would mean if it became serious. His mind was wandering like a spider on its web. He got up and walked around his living room, urinating several times in a few minutes. He took the phone, wanting to call another friend and ask if he had heard anything about Alex's problem. On second thought, he sat down and dropped the phone. He wanted to watch a television program but could not get himself together.

Ed accidentally dozed off on the sofa. Titi woke him up in the morning. "I didn't know you slept here," she said.

"I didn't mean to. I wanted to relax here for a little while before going to bed."

"It's already 6:00 a.m.," she said.

"Oh my goodness," he exclaimed. He rushed to take his shower. He did not want breakfast, but Titi intervened and insisted that he have his breakfast before leaving.

"I hope you'll survive these last days of the campaign," she said. "It will take a long time before we get out of this."

Ed didn't say anything before he left to meet his friends. The signs of worry could easily be read on his face, though he pretended that everything was fine. He called some of his friends on his way to the campaign office, most especially to ask about Alex's health.

It was at the office that he knew that it had been a false alarm—or, more accurately, that the story was exaggerated. Alex had gotten dehydrated during a meeting with his associates. He had sat down and asked for water, which had been given to him. He had drunk a little and continued with his activities after a good rest, and hoped for the best.

14

ELECTION DAY

VOTING

Almost everything about this election was history making. A great number of people came out to vote. Every speculation was that Alex would win by a landslide, although Ed was making fast inroads because of the students. The younger students, mostly those twenty or younger, wanted to vote only for the candidate who would make college or university fees cheaper or free, like Ed had promised. It seemed to be the most important agenda item for them. It was an idea that had come when the cost of education was becoming astronomical. Only a few, especially those from rich families, could get their education with little or no worry. Whoever offered free education, even if it wasn't attainable, was going to get the students' hearts.

However, there was division among the student leaders about whom to support. It was later revealed that some leaders invited Alex to the campuses to address the capricious trend of educational costs in the nation. Another group of the students' leaders who were ardently loyal to Alex's causes disagreed, and thought Alex had declared his position on those issues as part of his position on general national problems. Alex's supporters advised against his going to any campuses at the tail end of the campaign. Accepting that advice, Alex notified the student leaders who invited him that his tight schedule would not allow him to honor their invitations. Some of them accepted his excuse, whereas some others were enraged by his not coming.

His endurance under pressure coupled with building on the splendor and glory of his rally at the capital granted Alex a heroic achievement. A lot of people wished him to win. A few months earlier, he had not expected to find himself in such a position. It was not certain when Alex knew that things were changing in his favor, but the fundamental turnaround was the political and economic anger against politicians and all the people in the government. The grievances of the ordinary citizens turned from a soft wind into a fierce storm, and eventually to a hurricane that swept things away. People began to sigh with relief, saying they had eliminated the practice that created fear for their future. It was an unforeseen and unimaginable transition that would stir a profound and fundamental change of leadership in the country.

As the election results trickled in, emotion was high on both sides, mostly on the side of Ed, who made gigantic efforts to secure a lot of student support. However, some students who had been convinced by Alex's rhetoric at the rally had difficulty changing their minds. Those Alex fans maintained that the educational issues Ed had been mentioning lately had been adequately explained during the Capital National Park rally.

Both candidates were at their respective campaign headquarters waiting for the results. Counting was slower at some places than in some other places, mostly the rural areas. Anything that needed to be done was done, and there were no voter irregularities at any place. The early results from the cities with big university and college student populations showed Ed pulling ahead. When the results from the suburban areas and outside the cities started coming in, Ed's numbers started to tumble like a pack of cards.

When Ed finally realized that he was not going to win based on the total number of votes counted, he called Alex to congratulate him for his victory. "You are the president of our beautiful country. You have rewritten our history, and I wish you the best of luck. I will be available to serve my country in whichever capacity would suit your convenience. Good luck."

Alex thanked him and congratulated him on his maverick campaign. He assured Ed that he would not be lacking in his administration, having shown the nation that he had a big heart.

As Ed dropped his phone, Alex shed tears of joy. He didn't easily get emotional, but the instantaneous remembrance of his father and mother overwhelmed him, and he sobbed momentarily like a child. He wished they were alive. Sometimes, one couldn't avoid behaving like a child. He wished his parents were present to witness the incredible blessing to the family. He quietly got himself together and prepared to address his supporters.

Ed's Concession Speech

A few minutes after talking with the president-elect, Ed came out from his campaign headquarters to thank his supporters. A crowd was waiting for him, though they knew he was not getting the winning numbers. There was enthusiastic applause as he stepped out with his wife and children.

"Thank you, ladies and gentlemen," he began. "Anything that has a beginning must have an end. We have come to the conclusion of this election marathon. It has been a wonderful experience. I don't know where to start thanking each and every one of you for being there for me."

There was more applause.

"Let me first thank my dear wife and lovely children, who endured tremendously during this campaign. They have always been there for me. I appreciate that. The nature of this election made for pandemonium among the prospective candidates and our entire political system. Despite all the erratic reactions, I was able to come out with the full support of all my friends. My participation brought some sanity into this election and helped the citizens balance their democratic obligation by having choices. Extraordinary things happened, and I responded extraordinarily."

The crowd clapped again.

"We did not win, but we have built a bridge for the future. We are triumphant in every aspect of our efforts. The end of this road is the beginning of another."

There was more applause.

"With all the excitement and emotion, I want to especially thank my friends who started from day one, traveling with me through all the thorny terrains and roads. They exhausted every iota of energy in their bodies, left their families and jobs, and stood vigorously by me till the end. It was an enormous sacrifice. Such monumental affection continued to uplift me even when I thought I had come to the end of the sojourn. Although I am unable to reward you, I appreciate your love from the bottom of my heart."

The people responded with applause.

"One special request I want to make of you and the incoming administration is to invest in our children. I encountered some experiences that embittered my heart during this campaign. Some of the things that constitute our valor are eluding our children. We are manifesting a very narrow vision for them, irrespective of what we are saying to be politically correct. Anything that affects them affects the future of this country. At your best possible time and place and in the most convenient way, support children's programs, particularly those that support children with autism spectrum disorder. Some of you are novices when it comes to this disorder, like I was, but I can tell you that it has devastated our children at an alarming rate. Very soon, one out of ten children in this country will be autistic. Autism has no cure for now and affects all races and classes of families. A lot of us hear about it or see some of the children involved but do not comprehend what it's about. You are not alone. It is one of the blessings that came from this election. I learned a lot about these children that I didn't know before. Collectively, we can do more to uplift the hopes and expectations of our children in general."

People clapped again.

"As we all peacefully go home, I can't reiterate enough how you have made me proud. I am highly honored and will always lean on this formidable pillar. Every happening of life enriches our experiences. We can never be afraid to fall in life because of circumstances beyond our control, but courageously we must get up, dust ourselves off, and move forward. Thank you again and again, and God bless."

The applause lasted a long time.

15

THE RESULTS

The man who came to listen at a town hall meeting had involuntarily become a speaker and then a prospective candidate and had finally won the presidential election. The voting conformed with all the electoral rules and regulations. He had never been popular, but his charisma and power of speech had captivated his listeners and moved them to tears of hope during the rally. His plausible vision had blossomed like a sunflower, and people had graced it with pride and dignity. He was declared the president-elect, and the whole country went into jubilation and celebration. It was really a surge of excitement.

Before the final results were announced, a huge crowd of supporters and well-wishers had gathered around Alex's campaign headquarters. There was a roar of applause and cheers when it was announced that he had won the presidential election. It was like an amazing dream. He could not believe it himself, even when he had been congratulated by his opponent. He knelt down in his campaign headquarters, raised his hands high to thank God, and then bent down and kissed the floor. There was a lot of hugging from local leaders, campaign directors, and many others. There was a lot of clapping and singing outside the headquarters under a beautiful sky.

The Victory Speech

As Alex stepped out to make his victory speech, the applause was long and loud. "Thank you," he started.

There was more loud applause.

"First, let me thank the almighty God for blessing this day, and my family members, who felt the greatest heat of this campaign. Thank you, noble citizens of this beautiful country. Thank you, my supporters, friends, and compatriots. Your labors have been blessed. You all are the winners tonight. It is a wonderful feeling. This is really an unusual accomplishment, and I will treasure it dearly. This kind of victory has never happened before but was meant to happen, and was never predicted by the wise ones until it happened."

There was more applause.

"Thank you all for your uncompromising support. And my fullest gratitude to all of you who traveled around the country and spent sleepless nights to bring about this victory. It is a new day for me, for you, and for our beloved nation. All of you who voted, no matter for whom, are the hearts and pride of this nation. What you are experiencing today is the wonder of democracy."

The applause lasted a long time.

"Let me thank in a special way the organizers and those who attended the rally at Capital National Park. That was where this victory germinated."

The crowd clapped again.

"I want to thank you all again and again for your love and trust. You are exceptionally awesome. I am saying thank you because I don't have any better words to express my utmost gratitude. I cherish this honor and will hold it in profound reverence."

People cheered and clapped.

"I must confess that I never had the ambition to run for this office. But when the night seemed too long for my fellow citizens, tall walls thwarted every effort to see the light, and life seemed hopeless and like a miserable wreck, having someone stand up for them and do something or say something about the situation irrespective of the consequences became irresistible. When common things happen, uncommon things should be done to combat them if there is to be a change."

The applause was loud.

"Let me thank my father and my mother for blessed memories. They are my guardian angels. My mother, a prodigious genius and a profound symbol in my life, always blessed me and advised me to match my determination with my pursuits. When my father was here on earth, he was a visionary. He saw this victory and prophesied that I would be a great man. I didn't understand him. There wasn't anything special about my life or family that I thought could bring me fame. I just thought my loving father was wishing his son the best of luck. But everything has its time. The most significant thing my father told me when he was passing away, which was like a stamp on my palm, was that this world is a workshop and I should make my best out of it to produce something of uttermost value to myself and my nation. I owe it to him and my mother."

Again, there was loud applause.

"This is the highest pinnacle any citizen would dream to attain, irrespective of wealth or knowledge. This is a country where dreams are unlimited. It is the only place in this universe that has demonstrated that casting a vote is the profoundest symbol of democracy. The ritual is fundamental and sacred. We have to appraise this value in harmony with unrestrained and impregnable justification."

People responded by applauding.

"This is our dear country, and every hand must be on deck to make it what we want it to be. We can reach the heights no other nation could if we work together. You have designated me as your driver for the affairs of this nation, and you will not be disappointed. I will uplift everyone and make this generation and the generation to come better than anybody else would do."

The applause was loud.

"What I said during the rally at Capital National Park was not a promise but a commitment. I will use every drop of water and blood in my body to pursue those things and bring smiles to your faces."

This time there was not only applause but a song of praise.

"You have given me a mandate to be a president for everybody within the borders of this great nation, and I will make you proud for making this precious choice. Our core values must be maintained as necessary and with expediency."

Again the song of praise was sung.

"You have endured enough for a long time. The time has come to uplift our nation and renew your spirits so that you can prosper. Those who think that their future and chances of life are blighted should discard such feelings and embrace new ambition, hope, enthusiasm, and drive."

The applause was loud.

"I will address the nation at a better time. The welfare of this nation is in our hands. Every citizen and everyone who loves this beautiful nation must perform his or her part unselfishly. This is a two-way street: if this nation is going to protect you, you must protect this nation. If this nation is going to serve you, you must serve this nation effectively."

Applause broke out again.

"No more abandonment of our commitments to ourselves and to our people. No more self-seekers. The seat of progress, achievements, and modern civilization rests on your doing your task. A nation without vision perishes like a rotten vegetable. This nation will always be there for you, but will you be there for this nation always?"

"Yeeeeeeeeees!" the crowd roared.

"The greatness of this nation has been unmatched and unparalleled. I will advance the will of the people, their hopes and dreams. I have reached this position by extraordinary means in the history of this country, and I will achieve extraordinary things. Someone has to do the impossible for it to be possible. I will work untiringly for the interests of this country, and pursue success that will be hard to equal or repeat."

The cheers and songs were deafening.

"We have the momentum. We are strongly rooted, and determination is the master of progress. Though we are the greatest in the world, we have some missed opportunities that could be recuperated. Your hearts and minds are hungry to regain the status that made other nations tremble whenever and wherever our nation was mentioned."

The applause lasted a long time.

"From my humblest heart, I know we will achieve everything in our pursuit. In my conscience and light, I don't know all that God has for me, but I am certain he will work with me. God has always been kind to me and this nation. We are blessed because this nation is patented by God."

The applause was long and loud.

"It is necessary for every citizen and noncitizen in this country to perform for the good of the people. It is time to attack and combat all our problems irrespective of where any person comes from. You should be the first to get in front of this offensive for the best interests of our dear nation. Yes, you and all of us should."

The crowd cheered.

"This is a national feeling, a patriotic call, and you cannot harden your heart when you hear it. We are people of indissoluble unity and cannot be deaf when our nation calls. We are going to cultivate this land together so that we can harvest together."

The applause lasted several minutes as people rose to their feet.

"Our courage and sacrifices will never be weakened. We can feel the heart beat!"

"Yes, we can," roared the crowd.

"I will give this country a super-advanced quality of education, updating the educational curricula and adopting new technologies that have never been seen in this universe. I will assemble deep thinkers, illustrious teachers, and professors with the greatest knowledge on earth and pay them handsomely. Our nation's destiny is in our hands. We cannot claim to be great if our citizens do not feel the greatness."

The applause was loud.

"In this our own time, we are urged to establish pathways and manifestations of scientific greatness. Having been endowed with wealth and majesty, we are bound to make our nation more beautiful and rehabilitate where necessary."

There was more applause.

"Let me make it clear once again that this is the hour when we are called upon to serve our nation. You have to be the model strength that holds up your president so he can pursue his giant efforts. There is no place for personal triumph or distinction—only to be the worthiest ambassadors."

He was interrupted again by applause.

"Identifying yourself as a vessel of honor entails being the protector of this nation and the world in general. That will make you have sweet days to remember and proud moments in the history of this nation. Our ancient glories were the proud causes and sacrifices of our grandfathers and grandmothers."

The applause was long.

"This country is always moving forward and never backward. We always stand erect because we're a country that is proud but not arrogant about our might. I have faith in our citizens and their destinies. This is not a new creed or doctrine but what we inherited willingly from our ancestors. This government must procure all the necessities for the best interests of the people. Every endeavor is for the common glory of our nation. As we all have the need, there will be no postponement of our hopes and dreams. Either by provision or interpretation, wherever you have fear, there is hope."

The loud applause was followed by song.

"I have encountered a lot of odds in my life, and I have never been more resolute. Beyond any shadow of a doubt, nothing will undermine my determination. I am deeply conscious of the purpose and devotion of this office. This is a newness of life for our dear nation. This election has given me and the entire nation a proud victory beyond any imagination. I cannot conceal my gorgeous feelings."

The crowd clapped enthusiastically.

"I'm standing here now talking to you because of the prevalence of the citizens against the old way of doing our businesses. Our desires, whether old or new, will be the most expedient reason to take our nation to distant posterity. We must follow the tide or suffer the condemnation of history. Life is all about choices."

The applause was loud.

"Actually, our citizens do not demand much from our government: keep our parks and recreational places clean and healthy, and provide good roads and bridges, good-quality water and a clean environment, and advanced education and adequate security for our children. We want our police well equipped and given sufficient training, our military ever ready with tomorrow's technology, enough energy, and our industries running prominently with sophisticated machinery. We want the government to give all of them the tools they need to accomplish the warranted high expectations of them. People will be paying their taxes and keeping the financial institutions buoyant, and banks will be busy putting the money into circulation. Our entrepreneurs, merchants, and other citizens will have an unlimited range of opportunities to do their businesses. Everything is within our reach as long as we have a meeting of the minds. What else would you wish for this country?"

The applause lasted a long time.

"Let us lift up our hearts in this time of challenges to overcome our dissent, fears, and frustrations. Our citizens have always given their lives in different ways in times of crisis and danger. This unequaled affection for our country has granted us great honors at home and dignity abroad. We have been tested in several ways, and we always give testament to our ardent success. We are a nation of great potential, both dreamed and undreamed. Our neighboring countries have been fascinated with our potential, and our acquisitions have been envied."

There was tremendous applause.

"People came to this country to improve their lives and stayed thereafter because there was no better place to go. We welcome them because we have always been a generous nation. It has also been our culture and tradition to live together for the sake of peace. It is natural with our nation to aid others and make their lives better. If we sneezed, others would catch cold. That's why we are the finest."

The applause was accompanied by cheering.

"For the tranquility and orderliness of the world, we fight for other nations in times of need. We have always learned to live with our neighbors unless shown otherwise."

There were more cheers.

"Few people would think it a tremendous challenge to accomplish all our desires and expectations. You should be rest assured that I will honorably acknowledge such feelings, but as I said earlier, impossibility will one day be a possibility when someone breaks the barrier. Taking away greed, corruption, and self-seekers, we would achieve all this with a wave of hands. I will fight a war against unemployment, poverty, discrimination, unpatriotic feelings, and all the despair that eats into our national fabric. The guarantee is that something new is in the air. No labor is too hard and no journey is too long to bring happiness and pride to our country and citizens. You and I have been given a sense of purpose, inspiration, and direction. We have never been disappointed in the talents and ingeniousness of our people."

There was loud applause and song.

"This administration will soon publish the details of what will be done. We will hit the ground running from the first day. You must acknowledge the importance of collective efforts. To accomplish our dreams and imagination will not be my lone responsibility. The things that made us great were purchased with sacrifices—the sweat and blood of our patriots. They didn't ask to be rewarded with silver or gold, but they conquered for your prosperity. That's the instrument of our success."

Applause broke out once again.

"You are the jury tonight. If I am not speaking your mind, please raise your hand. I will wait a few seconds for a response."

The crowd was quiet, and no hands were raised.

"Thank you. Nobody raised their hand. Everything this administration pursues will be for our mutual benefit and for the greatness of our nation. Under no circumstances or contingencies should we allow others, not even our best friends, to determine our fate. I cannot shrink or back down until every line of action I pronounced tonight is judiciously accomplished. At the end of my tenure, you will see what I did with great passion and infinite tenderness."

Loud applause was followed by the national anthem.

"The task is heavy, but this is the government of the people, by the people, and for the people. We're going to task and tax our thoughts and pockets. Power to the people. Thanks to you all for voting and making me your choice. My special appreciation to all of you who went the extra distance to come down here to share this election result with me. I am indebted to every one of you jubilating here, and those rejoicing at your respective homes, offices, or other places. God willing, I will not disappoint you. Enjoy the rest of the night, and be peaceful."

Alex's speech was followed by several songs and a lot of jubilation.

SECURITY

Before Alex left, his supporters and surrogates continued to sing and fly their flags. The whole area was flooded with different kinds of national and local security agents, armed and unarmed, walking around with sophisticated communication gadgets. They were preventing people from getting too close to the president-elect. Military helicopters were hovering around the entire neighborhood. Alex the community man was no longer an ordinary citizen.

Printed in the United States
By Bookmasters